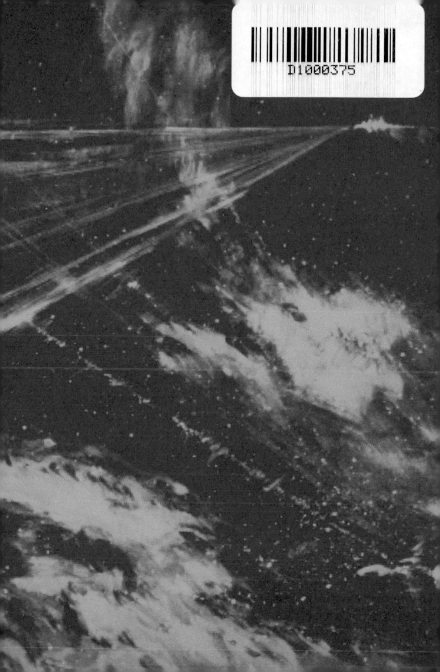

DATE DUE

APR 2 5 2005			

HOUSTON, HOUSTON, DO YOU READ?

JAMES TIPTREE, JR.

Illustrated by Bob Eggleton

INTRODUCTION

The 1970s, the decade in which the majority of the Tiptree stories were first published, saw the advent of feminism in science fiction, and Tiptree was one of the two writers with male names (the other was Samuel R. Delany) most involved in the feminist dialog that had moved to the center of the field by 1975. And it was clear that Tiptree was among the most popular and important writers to enter SF in the 70s. Feminism was the Movement, feminism was what was happening—it gave character to the decade, which was otherwise a period of new conservatism after the excitement and challenges of the New Wave controversies of the 1960s. And Tiptree wrote "The Women Men Don't See" (1973), one of the half-dozen or so most important feminist stories of the era, now a classic of the field. So you can imagine what a social explosion it was to find that he was a she.

James Tiptree, Jr., is the pseudonym most often used during the SF writing career of Alice Hastings Bradley Sheldon (1915–1987). Even after her identity was exposed in 1977, an event that sent shock waves throughout the SF field, she continued to refer to herself as Tip sometimes, though usually she used Allie.

She was Raccoona Sheldon, too. At a certain point she was so prolific and successful that she adopted a second pseudonym, as the old pulp writers did in the 1930s and 1940s, so that she could have two stories in the same anthology. It was in this way that "Houston, Houston, Do You Read?" was published as by Raccoona Sheldon in the paperback original anthology *Aurora: Beyond Equality*, edited by Vonda N. McIntyre and Susan J. Anderson, which also contained a Tiptree story. The anthology was a showcase of new feminist SF, and the Sheldon story got such attention that it won both a Hugo and a Nebula Award.

It is beyond the scope of this essay to pin down who Alice Sheldon really was. It is perhaps beyond my ability. She was a compelling storyteller, a charismatic person, a clinically depressed professor of psychology (she got her PHD in 1967). She was kind and extraordinarily generous, passionately involved in life, yet a person who first contemplated suicide as a child in India and in the end shot herself and her husband, for the love of whom she had stayed alive for at least a decade—she had promised him she would not kill herself while he was alive and well, but he had agreed to die when he became infirm.

She was an ex-employee of the Central Intelligence Agency, who had run away and hidden in order to resign in 1955. Her husband, Huntington Sheldon, was until his retirement a high official in that Agency, the man who had to approve the budget for all covert operations. She was an artist before WWII. Her first story was published in *The New Yorker* in 1946. She began, but never finished, a book on feminism in the early 1950s. She had secrets. She would drop narrative hooks into conversation such as "Someday maybe I'll be able to tell you how much trouble it was to get a urine sample from Khrushchev in the early 1960s, when we wanted to know about his health." No one, except perhaps the pseudonymous Cordwainer Smith (in real life Paul Linebarger, the man who wrote the basic text on psychological warfare and who remained professionally at the heart of the U.S. foreign service and intelligence community until his death in 1966), is as mysterious and romantic a figure in SF as James Tiptree, Jr.

The science fiction field began to notice Tiptree almost from the start. The story "The Last Flight of Dr. Ain" (1969) was a Nebula Award nominee, and in succeeding years Tiptree won many short fiction awards. Almost all of the stories from 1968 to 1978 are collected in four books: *Ten Thousand Light-Years from Home* (1973), *Warm Worlds and Otherwise* (1975), *Star Songs of an Old Primate* (1978) and *Out of the Everywhere and Other Extraordinary Visions* (1981). Tiptree was the most important writer to enter the SF field at the start of the 1970s, a mature talent, and was rapidly seen as a peer of the finest living writers. The next writer to cause a similar stir, later in the 1970s, was John Varley.

I became the editor of her novels in 1977, at about the time her identity was revealed. Her novel, *Up the Walls of the World* (1978), had been finished for another editor, Judy Lynn del Rey, who then rejected it. I was delighted to publish it. But it happened at the time that Tiptree's real identity had just been revealed and at that movement Allie Sheldon found she couldn't write SF any more—for a time. The revelation of her true identity had stripped her of a carefully constructed persona with which she was comfortable. Now she was at a loss. For several years her writing slowed from a flood to a trickle. I went to her home for a day in 1977 to drop off a Nebula Award she had won. It was an extraordinary afternoon, during which she talked a blue streak and was a perfect hostess. It cost her a great effort, though—the subject of dinner had been broached, but Ting took me aside and said not to stay. "It'll take her days to recover." They were a courtly and romantic couple, giving every evidence of being extremely close and loving. She often told her friends she was thinking about killing herself, but with a charming, ironic tone, as if talking to you banished the thought.

She remained enchanting even when little new fiction appeared, a public figure of immense stature, though she never once appeared in public, communicating only by phone and by letter. She was an active and voluminous correspondent, always kind and supportive to younger writers, and a crucial figure for women in science fiction. When she finished her second novel I was out of work, but she sent it to me anyway, at home. She had decided I was her editor. So I edited it with her and when I got a job the next year, bought and published *Brightness Falls From the Air* (1985). I edited her last story collections, *The Starry Rift* (1986) and *Crown of Stars* (1988) after that.

She wrote tragic science fiction, and no matter whether her stories were feminist or concerned with ecology and the environment—often both—she always wrote about death. She was also a moralist, and a complex one, in the end hard to pin down. Tiptree's vision was a very dark vision of life, and of the human condition, filled with horrifying moments of discovery.

Her influence has persisted. Her early story, "Beam Us Home," is still in my opinion the best story ever written about Star Trek—without once mentioning the name. In the 1980s her story "The Girl Who Was Plugged In" (1973) was acknowledged by William Gibson as one of the origins of cyberpunk in SF. And in the newer generations of women in science fiction, a group led by Pat Murphy and Karen Joy Fowler founded the James Tiptree, Jr. Award, given annually by a jury, "for gender-bending science fiction." It is a lively and unconventional award (the trophy is made of chocolate; the ceremony is supported by bake sales at conventions around the country) and is succeeding in focussing more attention on feminist SF in the 1990s.

"Houston, Houston, Do You Read?" was a stunning story when it first appeared, and although we are not perhaps so shocked by some of the ideas as the 1977 audience, it still has substantial power. It is of course directly and intentionally a feminist story, and has been called a utopian story, though I do not agree. It is certainly written to upset readers with unthinking prejudices about sex, race, gender roles. On that level it appeals emotionally, and it seems particularly clever to have told it from the point of view of a good man torn from his culture and burdened with gender-role guilt, and to require him to witness with horror the loathsome acting out of his comrades (which the women observe with clinical detachment and relative good humor). In that sense it is perhaps too artificial a set-up, a lurid allegory of good women and bad men—though it is *his* interpretation.

But I see it even more in the tradition of the famous Tom Godwin story, "The Cold Equations," in which logic demands human sacrifice. And there remains the intriguing question of who is sacrificing whom and for what?

Lorimer may not foresee it, but if we read carefully we know he is going to survive and return to his own time, because he is one of the founders of the world of the future, his name is on a plaque. And there is one line in the story I find endlessly puzzling, when the men are first contacting the women to be rescued: "We did not mention our epidemic."

This is not a story to be exhausted by a few facile lines of interpretation, it is a living story to be experienced. It was written by a woman who loved art, and her husband, and the world. Perhaps she behaved badly in the end. The mystery of who she was remains, and the stories, her legacy.

—David G. Hartwell
Pleasantville, N.Y.

HOUSTON, HOUSTON, DO YOU READ?

Lorimer gazes around the crowded cabin, trying to listen to the voices, trying to ignore the twitch in his insides that means he is about to remember something bad. No help; he lives it again, that long-ago moment. Himself running blindly—or was he pushed?—into the strange toilet at Evanston Junior High. His fly open, his dick in his hand, he can still see the gray zipper edge of his jeans around his pale exposed pecker. The hush. The sickening wrongness of shapes, faces turning. The first blaring giggle. *Girls.* He was in the *girls' can.*

He flinches now wryly, so many years later, not looking at the women's faces. The big cabin surrounds him with their alien things, curved around over his head: the beading rack, the twins' loom, Andy's leatherwork, the damned kudzu vine wriggling everywhere, the chickens. So cozy. . . . Trapped, he is. Irretriev-

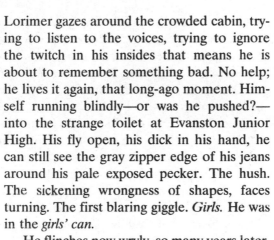

1

ably trapped for life in everything he does not enjoy. Structurelessness. Personal trivia, unmeaning intimacies. The claims he can somehow never meet. Ginny: *You never talk to me* . . . Ginny, love, he thinks involuntarily. The hurt doesn't come.

Bud Geirr's loud chuckle breaks in on him. Bud is joking with some of them, out of sight around a bulkhead. Dave is visible, though. Major Norman Davis on the far side of the cabin, his bearded profile bent toward a small dark woman Lorimer can't quite focus on. But Dave's head seems oddly tiny and sharp, in fact the whole cabin looks unreal. A cackle bursts out from the "ceiling"—the bantam hen in her basket.

At this moment Lorimer becomes sure he has been drugged.

Curiously, the idea does not anger him. He leans or rather tips back, perching cross-

2

legged in the zero gee, letting his gaze go to the face of the woman he has been talking with. Connie. Constantia Morelos. A tall moon-faced woman in capacious green pajamas. He has never really cared for talking to women. Ironic.

"I suppose," he says aloud, "it's possible that in some sense we are not here."

That doesn't sound too clear, but she nods interestedly. She's watching my reactions, Lorimer tells himself. Women are natural poisoners. Has he said that aloud, too? Her expression doesn't change. His vision is taking on a pleasing local clarity. Connie's skin strikes him as quite fine, healthy-looking. Olive tan even after two years in space. She was a farmer, he recalls. Big pores, but without the caked look he associates with women her age.

"You probably never wore makeup," he

3

says. She looks puzzled. "Face paint, powder. None of you have."

"Oh!" Her smile shows a chipped front tooth. "Oh yes, I think Andy has."

"Andy?"

"For plays. Historical plays, Andy's good at that."

"Of course. Historical plays."

Lorimer's brain seems to be expanding, letting in light. He is understanding actively now, the myriad bits and pieces linking into patterns. Deadly patterns, he perceives; but the drug is shielding him in some way. Like an amphetamine high without the pressure. Maybe it's something they use socially? No, they're watching, too.

"Space bunnies, I still don't dig it," Bud Geirr laughs infectiously. He has a friendly buoyant voice people like; Lorimer still likes it after two years.

4

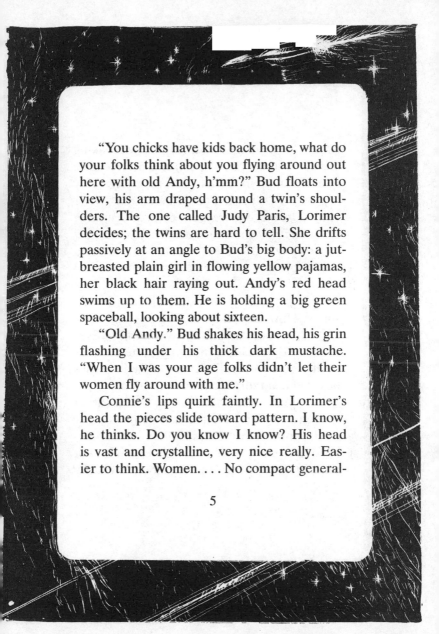

"You chicks have kids back home, what do your folks think about you flying around out here with old Andy, h'mm?" Bud floats into view, his arm draped around a twin's shoulders. The one called Judy Paris, Lorimer decides; the twins are hard to tell. She drifts passively at an angle to Bud's big body: a jut-breasted plain girl in flowing yellow pajamas, her black hair raying out. Andy's red head swims up to them. He is holding a big green spaceball, looking about sixteen.

"Old Andy." Bud shakes his head, his grin flashing under his thick dark mustache. "When I was your age folks didn't let their women fly around with me."

Connie's lips quirk faintly. In Lorimer's head the pieces slide toward pattern. I know, he thinks. Do you know I know? His head is vast and crystalline, very nice really. Easier to think. Women. . . . No compact general-

5

ization forms in his mind, only a few speaking faces on a matrix of pervasive irrelevance. Human, of course. Biological necessity. Only so, so . . . diffuse? Pointless? . . . His sister Amy, *soprano con tremulo: Of course women could contribute as much as men if you'd treat us as equals. You'll see!* And then marrying that idiot the second time. Well, now he can see.

"Kudzu vines," he says aloud. Connie smiles. How they all smile.

"How 'boot that?" Bud says happily. "Ever think we'd see chicks in zero gee, hey, Dave? Artits-stico. Woo-ee!" Across the cabin Dave's bearded head turns to him, not smiling.

"And ol' Andy's had it all to hisself. Stunt your growth, lad." He punches Andy genially on the arm, Andy catches himself on the bulkhead. Bud can't be drunk, Lorimer thinks; not on that fruit cider. But he doesn't usually sound so much like a stage Texan either. A drug.

"Hey, no offense," Bud is saying earnestly to the boy, "I mean that. You have to forgive one underprilly, underprivileged brother. These chicks are good people. Know what?" he tells the girl. "You could look stu-pen-dous if you fix yourself up a speck. Hey, I can show you, old Buddy's a expert. I hope you don't mind my saying that. As a matter of fact you look real stupendous to me right now."

He hugs her shoulders, flings out his arm and hugs Andy, too. They float upwards in his grasp, Judy grinning excitedly, almost pretty.

"Let's get some more of that good stuff." Bud propels them both toward the serving rack which is decorated for the occasion with sprays of greens and small real daisies.

"Happy New Year! Hey, Happy New Year, y'all!"

7

Faces turn, more smiles. Genuine smiles, Lorimer thinks, maybe they really like their New Years. He feels he has infinite time to examine every event, the implications evolving in crystal facets. I'm an echo chamber. Enjoyable, to be the observer. But others are observing, too. They've started something here. Do they realize? So vulnerable, three of us, five of them in this fragile ship. They don't know. A dread unconnected to action lurks behind his mind.

"By God, we made it," Bud laughs. "You space chickies, I have to give it to you. I commend you, by God, I say it. We wouldn't be here, wherever we are. Know what, I jus' might decide to stay in the service after all. Think they have room for old Bud in your space program, sweetie?"

"Knock that off, Bud," Dave says quietly from the far wall. "I don't want to hear us use

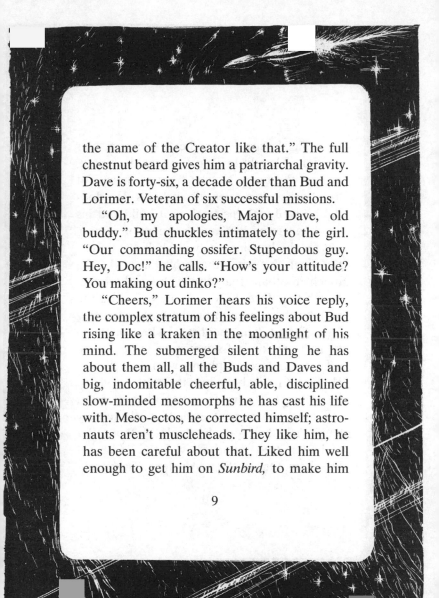

the name of the Creator like that." The full
chestnut beard gives him a patriarchal gravity.
Dave is forty-six, a decade older than Bud and
Lorimer. Veteran of six successful missions.

"Oh, my apologies, Major Dave, old
buddy." Bud chuckles intimately to the girl.
"Our commanding ossifer. Stupendous guy.
Hey, Doc!" he calls. "How's your attitude?
You making out dinko?"

"Cheers," Lorimer hears his voice reply,
the complex stratum of his feelings about Bud
rising like a kraken in the moonlight of his
mind. The submerged silent thing he has
about them all, all the Buds and Daves and
big, indomitable cheerful, able, disciplined
slow-minded mesomorphs he has cast his life
with. Meso-ectos, he corrected himself; astronauts aren't muscleheads. They like him, he
has been careful about that. Liked him well
enough to get him on *Sunbird,* to make him

9

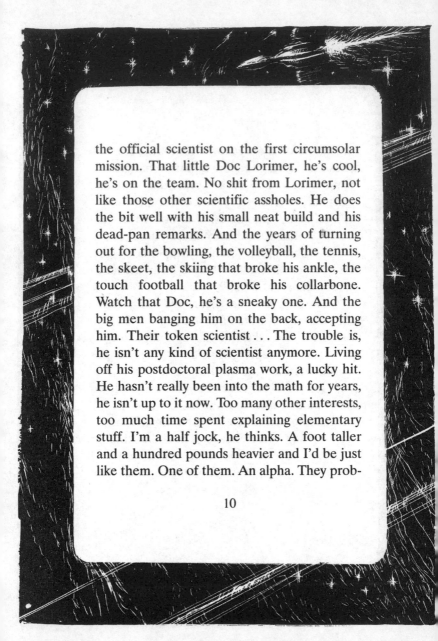

the official scientist on the first circumsolar
mission. That little Doc Lorimer, he's cool,
he's on the team. No shit from Lorimer, not
like those other scientific assholes. He does
the bit well with his small neat build and his
dead-pan remarks. And the years of turning
out for the bowling, the volleyball, the tennis,
the skeet, the skiing that broke his ankle, the
touch football that broke his collarbone.
Watch that Doc, he's a sneaky one. And the
big men banging him on the back, accepting
him. Their token scientist . . . The trouble is,
he isn't any kind of scientist anymore. Living
off his postdoctoral plasma work, a lucky hit.
He hasn't really been into the math for years,
he isn't up to it now. Too many other interests,
too much time spent explaining elementary
stuff. I'm a half jock, he thinks. A foot taller
and a hundred pounds heavier and I'd be just
like them. One of them. An alpha. They prob-

10

ably sense it underneath, the beta bile. Had the jokes worn a shade thin in *Sunbird,* all that year going out? A year of Bud and Dave playing gin. That damn exercycle, gearing it up too tough for me. They didn't mean it, though. We were a team.

The memory of gaping jeans flicks at him, the painful end part—the grinning faces waiting for him when he stumbled out. The howls, the dribble down his leg. Being cool, pretending to laugh, too. You shitheads, I'll show you. I am not a girl.

Bud's voice rings out, chanting. "And a Hap-pee New Year to you-all down there!" Parody of the oily NASA tone. "Hey, why don't we shoot 'em a signal? Greetings to all you Earthlings, I mean, all you little Lunies. Hap-py New Year in the good year whatsis." He snuffles comically. "There is a Santy Claus, Houston, ye-ew nevah saw nothin' like this!

11

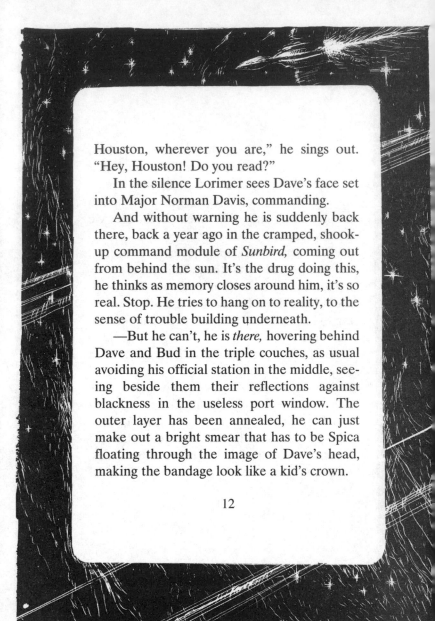

Houston, wherever you are," he sings out. "Hey, Houston! Do you read?"

In the silence Lorimer sees Dave's face set into Major Norman Davis, commanding.

And without warning he is suddenly back there, back a year ago in the cramped, shook-up command module of *Sunbird,* coming out from behind the sun. It's the drug doing this, he thinks as memory closes around him, it's so real. Stop. He tries to hang on to reality, to the sense of trouble building underneath.

—But he can't, he is *there,* hovering behind Dave and Bud in the triple couches, as usual avoiding his official station in the middle, seeing beside them their reflections against blackness in the useless port window. The outer layer has been annealed, he can just make out a bright smear that has to be Spica floating through the image of Dave's head, making the bandage look like a kid's crown.

12

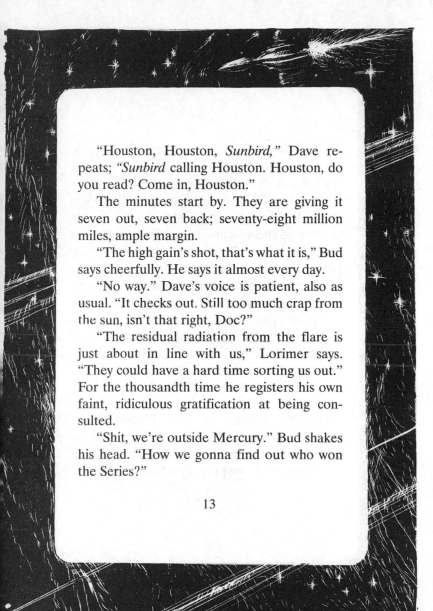

"Houston, Houston, *Sunbird*," Dave repeats; "*Sunbird* calling Houston. Houston, do you read? Come in, Houston."

The minutes start by. They are giving it seven out, seven back; seventy-eight million miles, ample margin.

"The high gain's shot, that's what it is," Bud says cheerfully. He says it almost every day.

"No way." Dave's voice is patient, also as usual. "It checks out. Still too much crap from the sun, isn't that right, Doc?"

"The residual radiation from the flare is just about in line with us," Lorimer says. "They could have a hard time sorting us out." For the thousandth time he registers his own faint, ridiculous gratification at being consulted.

"Shit, we're outside Mercury." Bud shakes his head. "How we gonna find out who won the Series?"

13

He often says that, too. A ritual, out here in eternal night. Lorimer watches the sparkle of Spica drift by the reflection of Bud's curly facebush. His own whiskers are scant and scraggly, like a blond Fu Manchu. In the aft corner of the window is a striped glare that must be the remains of their port energy accumulators, fried off in the solar explosion that hit them a month ago and fused the outer layers of their windows. That was when Dave cut his head open on the sexlogic panel. Lorimer had been banged in among the gravity wave experiment, he still doesn't trust the readings. Luckily the particle stream has missed one piece of the front window; they still have about twenty degrees of clear vision straight ahead. The brilliant web of the Pleiades shows there, running off into a blur of light.

Twelve minutes . . . thirteen. The speaker sighs and clicks emptily. Fourteen. Nothing.

14

"*Sunbird* to Houston, *Sunbird* to Houston. Come in, Houston. *Sunbird* out." Dave puts the mike back in its holder. "Give it another twenty-four."

They wait ritually. Tomorrow Packard will reply. Maybe.

"Be good to see old Earth again," Bud remarks.

"We're not using any more fuel on attitude," Dave reminds him. "I trust Doc's figures."

It's not my figures, it's the elementary facts of celestial mechanics, Lorimer thinks; in October there's only one place for Earth to be. He never says it. Not to a man who can fly two-body solutions by intuition once he knows where the bodies are. Bud is a good pilot and a better engineer; Dave is the best there is. He takes no pride in it. "The Lord helps us, Doc, if we let Him."

15

"Going to be a bitch docking if the radar's screwed up," Bud says idly. They all think about that for the hundredth time. It will be a bitch. Dave will do it. That was why he is hoarding fuel.

The minutes tick off.

"That's it," Dave says—and a voice fills the cabin, shockingly.

"Judy?" It is high and clear. A girl's voice.

"Judy, I'm so glad we got you. What are you doing on this band?"

Bud blows out his breath; there is a frozen instant before Dave snatches up the mike.

Sunbird, we read you. This is Mission *Sunbird* calling Houston, ah, *Sunbird One* calling Houston Ground Control. Identify, who are you? Can you relay our signal? Over."

"Some skip," Bud says. "Some incredible ham."

"Are you in trouble, Judy?" the girl's voice

16

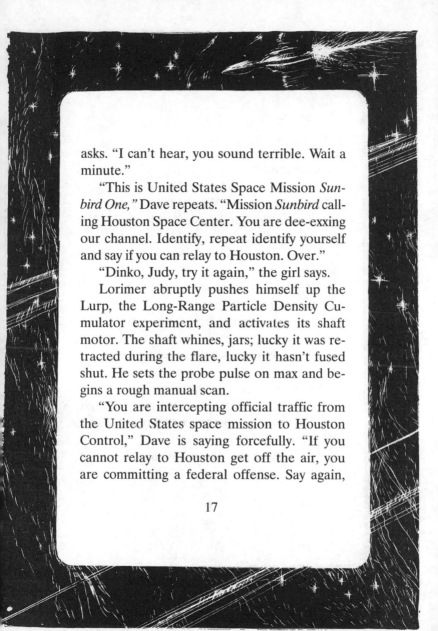

asks. "I can't hear, you sound terrible. Wait a minute."

"This is United States Space Mission *Sunbird One,*" Dave repeats. "Mission *Sunbird* calling Houston Space Center. You are dee-exxing our channel. Identify, repeat identify yourself and say if you can relay to Houston. Over."

"Dinko, Judy, try it again," the girl says.

Lorimer abruptly pushes himself up the Lurp, the Long-Range Particle Density Cumulator experiment, and activates its shaft motor. The shaft whines, jars; lucky it was retracted during the flare, lucky it hasn't fused shut. He sets the probe pulse on max and begins a rough manual scan.

"You are intercepting official traffic from the United States space mission to Houston Control," Dave is saying forcefully. "If you cannot relay to Houston get off the air, you are committing a federal offense. Say again,

17

can you relay our signal to Houston Space Center? Over."

"You still sound terrible," the girl says. "What's Houston? Who's talking, anyway? You know we don't have much time." Her voice is sweet but very nasal.

"Jesus, that's close," Bud says. "That is close."

"Hold it." Dave twists around to Lorimer's improvised radarscope.

"There." Lorimer points out a tiny stable peak at the extreme edge of the read-out slot, in the transcoronal scatter. Bud cranes too.

"A bogey!"

"Somebody else out here."

"Hello, hello? We have you now," the girl says. "Why are you so far out? Are you dinko, did you catch the flare?"

"Hold it," warns Dave. "What's the status, Doc?"

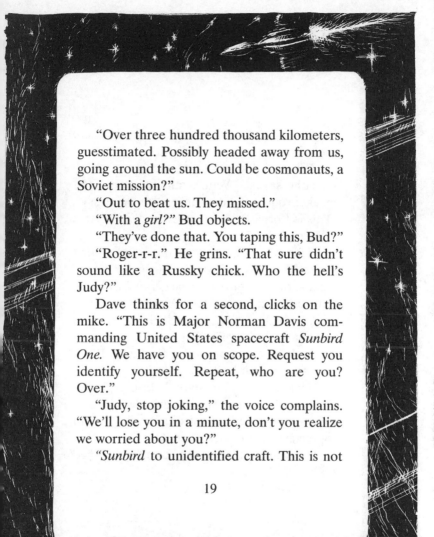

"Over three hundred thousand kilometers, guesstimated. Possibly headed away from us, going around the sun. Could be cosmonauts, a Soviet mission?"

"Out to beat us. They missed."

"With a *girl?*" Bud objects.

"They've done that. You taping this, Bud?"

"Roger-r-r." He grins. "That sure didn't sound like a Russky chick. Who the hell's Judy?"

Dave thinks for a second, clicks on the mike. "This is Major Norman Davis commanding United States spacecraft *Sunbird One.* We have you on scope. Request you identify yourself. Repeat, who are you? Over."

"Judy, stop joking," the voice complains. "We'll lose you in a minute, don't you realize we worried about you?"

"Sunbird to unidentified craft. This is not

19

Judy. I say again, this is not Judy. Who are you? Over."

"What—" the girl says, and is cut off by someone saying, "Wait a minute, Ann." The speaker squeals. Then a different woman says, "This is Lorna Bethune in *Escondita*. What is going on here?"

"This is Major Davis commanding United States Mission *Sunbird* on course for Earth. We do not recognize any spacecraft *Escondita*. Will you identify yourself? Over."

"I just did." She sounds older with the same nasal drawl. "There is no spaceship *Sunbird* and you're not on course for Earth. If this is an andy joke it isn't any good."

"This is no joke, madam!" Dave explodes. "This is the American circumsolar mission and we are American astronauts. We do not appreciate your interference. Out."

The woman starts to speak and is drowned

20

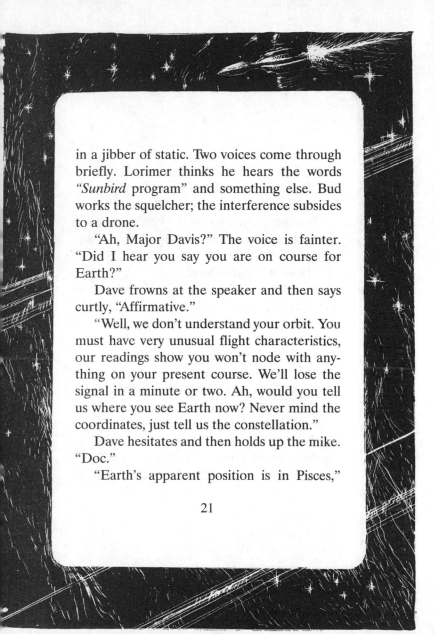

in a jibber of static. Two voices come through briefly. Lorimer thinks he hears the words *"Sunbird* program" and something else. Bud works the squelcher; the interference subsides to a drone.

"Ah, Major Davis?" The voice is fainter. "Did I hear you say you are on course for Earth?"

Dave frowns at the speaker and then says curtly, "Affirmative."

"Well, we don't understand your orbit. You must have very unusual flight characteristics, our readings show you won't node with anything on your present course. We'll lose the signal in a minute or two. Ah, would you tell us where you see Earth now? Never mind the coordinates, just tell us the constellation."

Dave hesitates and then holds up the mike. "Doc."

"Earth's apparent position is in Pisces,"

21

Lorimer says to the voice. "Approximately three degrees from P. Gamma."

"It is not," the woman says. "Can't you see it's in Virgo? Can't you see out at all?"

Lorimer's eyes go to the bright smear in the port window. "We sustained some damage—"

"Hold it," snaps Dave.

"—to one window during a disturbance we ran into at perihelion. Naturally we know the relative direction of Earth on this date, October nineteen."

"October? It's March, March fifteen. You must—" Her voice is lost in a shriek.

"E-M front," Bud says, tuning. They are all leaning at the speaker from different angles, Lorimer is head-down. Space noise wails and crashes like surf, the strange ship is too close to the coronal horizon. "—Behind you," they hear. More howls. "Band, try . . . ship . . . if

22

you can, your signal—" Nothing more comes through.

Lorimer pushes back, staring at the spark in the window. It has to be Spica. But is it elongated, as if a second point-source is beside it? Impossible. An excitement is trying to flare out inside him, the women's voices resonate in his head.

"Playback," Dave says. "Houston will really like to hear this."

They listen again to the girl calling Judy, the woman saying she is Lorna Bethune. Bud holds up a finger. "Man's voice in there." Lorimer listens hard for the words he thought he heard. The tape ends.

"Wait till Packard gets this one." Dave rubs his arms. "Remember what they pulled on Howie? Claiming they rescued him."

"Seems like they want us on their frequency." Bud grins. "They must think we're

23

fa-a-ar gone. Hey, looks like this other capsule's going to show up, getting crowded out here."

"If it shows up," Dave says. "Leave it on voice alert, Bud. The batteries will do that."

Lorimer watches the spark of Spica, or Spica-plus-something, wondering if he will ever understand. The casual acceptance of some trick or ploy out here in this incredible loneliness. Well, if these strangers are from the same mold, maybe that is it. Aloud he says, *"Escondita* is an odd name for a Soviet mission. I believe it means 'hidden' in Spanish."

"Yeah," says Bud. "Hey, I know what that accent is, it's Australian. We had some Aussie bunnies at Hickam. Or-stryle-ya, woo-ee! You s'pose Woomara is sending up some kind of com-bined do?"

Dave shakes his head. "They have no capability whatsoever."

24

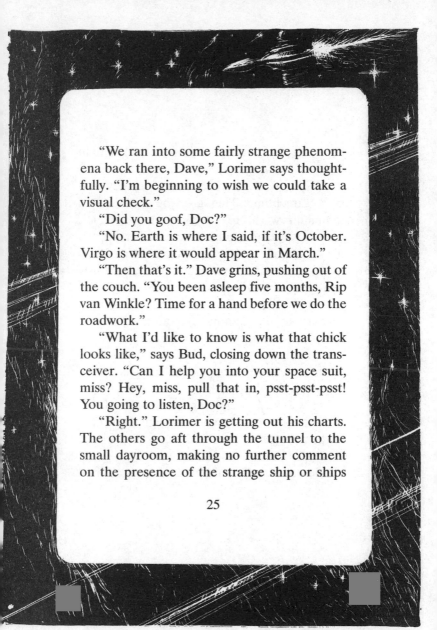

"We ran into some fairly strange phenomena back there, Dave," Lorimer says thoughtfully. "I'm beginning to wish we could take a visual check."

"Did you goof, Doc?"

"No. Earth is where I said, if it's October. Virgo is where it would appear in March."

"Then that's it." Dave grins, pushing out of the couch. "You been asleep five months, Rip van Winkle? Time for a hand before we do the roadwork."

"What I'd like to know is what that chick looks like," says Bud, closing down the transceiver. "Can I help you into your space suit, miss? Hey, miss, pull that in, psst-psst-psst! You going to listen, Doc?"

"Right." Lorimer is getting out his charts. The others go aft through the tunnel to the small dayroom, making no further comment on the presence of the strange ship or ships

25

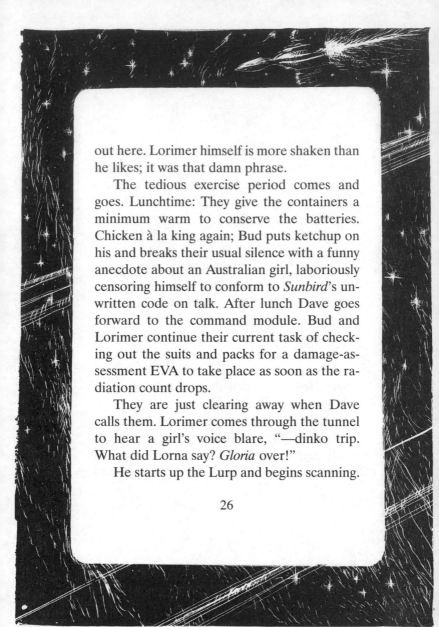

out here. Lorimer himself is more shaken than he likes; it was that damn phrase.

The tedious exercise period comes and goes. Lunchtime: They give the containers a minimum warm to conserve the batteries. Chicken à la king again; Bud puts ketchup on his and breaks their usual silence with a funny anecdote about an Australian girl, laboriously censoring himself to conform to *Sunbird*'s unwritten code on talk. After lunch Dave goes forward to the command module. Bud and Lorimer continue their current task of checking out the suits and packs for a damage-assessment EVA to take place as soon as the radiation count drops.

They are just clearing away when Dave calls them. Lorimer comes through the tunnel to hear a girl's voice blare, "—dinko trip. What did Lorna say? *Gloria* over!"

He starts up the Lurp and begins scanning.

26

No results this time. "They're either in line behind us or in the sunward quadrant," he reports finally. "I can't isolate them."

Presently the speaker holds another thin thread of sound.

"That could be their ground control," says Dave. "How's the horizon, Doc?"

"Five hours; Northwest Siberia, Japan, Australia."

"I told you the high gain is fucked up." Bud gingerly feeds power to his antenna motor. "Easy, eas-ee. The frame is twisted, that's what it is."

"Don't snap it," Dave says, knowing Bud will not.

The squeaking fades, pulses back. "Hey, we can really use this," Bud says. "We can calibrate on them."

A hard soprano says suddenly "—should be outside your orbit. Try around Beta Aries."

27

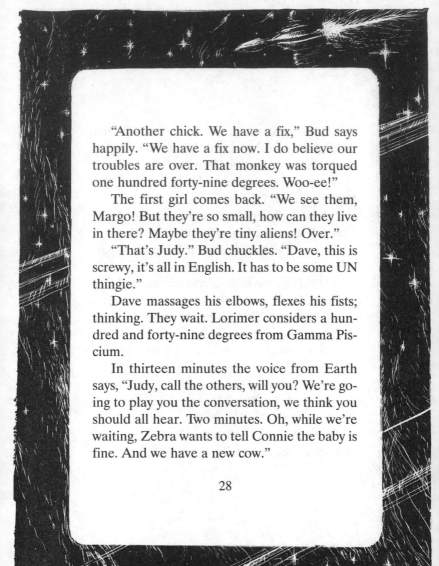

"Another chick. We have a fix," Bud says happily. "We have a fix now. I do believe our troubles are over. That monkey was torqued one hundred forty-nine degrees. Woo-ee!"

The first girl comes back. "We see them, Margo! But they're so small, how can they live in there? Maybe they're tiny aliens! Over."

"That's Judy." Bud chuckles. "Dave, this is screwy, it's all in English. It has to be some UN thingie."

Dave massages his elbows, flexes his fists; thinking. They wait. Lorimer considers a hundred and forty-nine degrees from Gamma Piscium.

In thirteen minutes the voice from Earth says, "Judy, call the others, will you? We're going to play you the conversation, we think you should all hear. Two minutes. Oh, while we're waiting, Zebra wants to tell Connie the baby is fine. And we have a new cow."

28

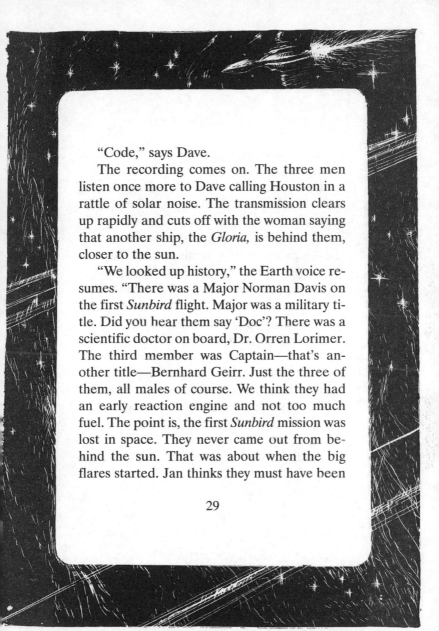

"Code," says Dave.

The recording comes on. The three men listen once more to Dave calling Houston in a rattle of solar noise. The transmission clears up rapidly and cuts off with the woman saying that another ship, the *Gloria*, is behind them, closer to the sun.

"We looked up history," the Earth voice resumes. "There was a Major Norman Davis on the first *Sunbird* flight. Major was a military title. Did you hear them say 'Doc'? There was a scientific doctor on board, Dr. Orren Lorimer. The third member was Captain—that's another title—Bernhard Geirr. Just the three of them, all males of course. We think they had an early reaction engine and not too much fuel. The point is, the first *Sunbird* mission was lost in space. They never came out from behind the sun. That was about when the big flares started. Jan thinks they must have been

29

close to one, you heard them say they were damaged."

Dave grunts. Lorimer is fighting excitement like a brush discharge sparking in his gut.

"Either they are who they say they are or they're ghosts; or they're aliens pretending to be people. Jan says maybe the disruption in those super-flares could collapse the local time dimension. Pluggo. What did you observe there, I mean the highlights?"

Time dimension ... never come back ... Lorimer's mind narrows onto the reality of the two unmoving bearded heads before him, refuses to admit the words he thought he heard: *Before the year two thousand.* The language, he thinks. The language would have to have changed. He feels better.

A deep baritone voice says, "Margo?" In *Sunbird* eyes come alert.

30

"—like the big one fifty years ago." The man has the accent, too. "We were really lucky being right there when it popped. The most interesting part is that we confirmed the gravity turbulence. Periodic but not waves. It's violent, we got pushed around some. Space is under monster stress in those things. We think France's theory that our system is passing through a micro-black-hole cluster looks right so long as one doesn't plonk us."

"France?" Bud mutters. Dave looks at him speculatively.

"It's hard to imagine anything being kicked out in time. But they're here, whatever they are, they're over eight hundred kays outside us scooting out toward Aldebaran. As Lorna said, if they're trying to reach Earth they're in trouble unless they have a lot of spare gecs. Should we try to talk to them? Over. Oh, great about the cow. Over again."

31

"Black holes." Bud whistles softly. "That's one for you, Doc. Was we in a black hole?"

"Not in one or we wouldn't be here." If we are here, Lorimer adds to himself. A micro-black-hole cluster . . . what happens when fragments of totally collapsed matter approach each other, or collide, say in the photosphere of a star? Time disruption? Stop it. Aloud he says, "They could be telling us something, Dave."

Dave says nothing. The minutes pass.

Finally the Earth voice comes back, saying that it will try to contact the strangers on their original frequency. Bud glances at Dave, tunes the selector.

"Calling *Sunbird One?*" the girl says slowly through her nose. "This is Luna Central calling Major Norman Davis of *Sunbird One.* We have picked up your conversation with our ship *Escondita.* We are very puzzled as to who you are and how you got here. If you really are *Sunbird One* we think you must have been jumped forward in time when you passed the solar flare." She pronounces it Cockney style, "toime."

"Our ship *Gloria* is near you, they see you on their radar. We think you may have a serious course problem because you told Lorna you were headed for Earth and you think it is now October with Earth in Pisces. It is not October. It is March fifteen. I repeat, the Earth date"—she says "dyte"—"is March fifteen, time twenty hundred hours. You should be able to see Earth very close to Spica in Virgo. You said your window is damaged. Can't you go out and look? We think you have to make a big course correction. Do you have enough fuel? Do you have a computer? Do you have enough air and water and food? Can we help you? We're listening on

33

this frequency. Luna to *Sunbird One,* come in."

On *Sunbird* nobody stirs. Lorimer struggles against internal eruptions. *Never came back. Jumped forward in time.* The cyst of memories he has schooled himself to suppress bulges up in the lengthening silence. "Aren't you going to answer?"

"Don't be stupid," Dave says.

"Dave. A hundred and forty-nine degrees is the difference between Gamma Piscium and Spica. That transmission is coming from where they say Earth is."

"You goofed."

"I did not goof. It has to be March."

Dave blinks as if a fly is bothering him.

In fifteen minutes the Luna voice runs through the whole thing again, ending, "Please, come in."

"Not a tape." Bud unwraps a stick of gum,

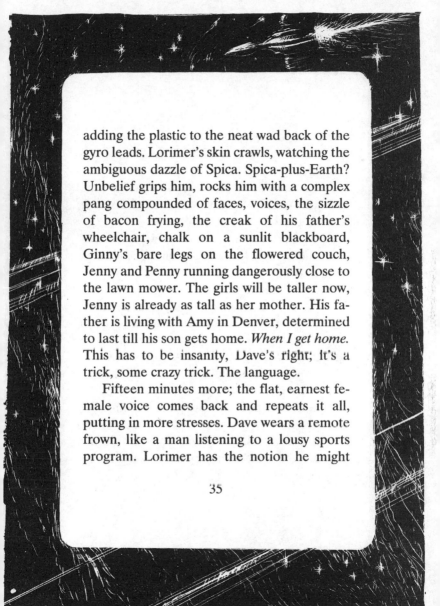

adding the plastic to the neat wad back of the gyro leads. Lorimer's skin crawls, watching the ambiguous dazzle of Spica. Spica-plus-Earth? Unbelief grips him, rocks him with a complex pang compounded of faces, voices, the sizzle of bacon frying, the creak of his father's wheelchair, chalk on a sunlit blackboard, Ginny's bare legs on the flowered couch, Jenny and Penny running dangerously close to the lawn mower. The girls will be taller now, Jenny is already as tall as her mother. His father is living with Amy in Denver, determined to last till his son gets home. *When I get home.* This has to be insanity, Dave's right; it's a trick, some crazy trick. The language.

Fifteen minutes more; the flat, earnest female voice comes back and repeats it all, putting in more stresses. Dave wears a remote frown, like a man listening to a lousy sports program. Lorimer has the notion he might

35

switch off and propose a hand of gin; wills him to do so. The voice says it will now change frequencies.

Bud tunes back, chewing calmly. This time the voice stumbles on a couple of phrases. It sounds tired.

Another wait; an hour, now. Lorimer's mind holds only the bright point of Spica digging at him. Bud hums a bar of "Yellow Ribbons," falls silent again.

"Dave," Lorimer says finally, "our antenna is pointed straight at Spica. I don't care if you think I goofed, if Earth is over there we have to change course soon. Look, you can see it could be a double light source. We have to check this out."

Dave says nothing. Bud says nothing but his eyes rove to the port window, back to his instrument panel, to the window again. In the corner of the panel is a polaroid snap of his

36

wife. Patty: a tall, giggling, rump-switching redhead; Lorimer has occasional fantasies about her. Little-girl voice, though. And so tall. . . . Some short men chase tall women; it strikes Lorimer as undignified. Ginny is an inch shorter than he. Their girls will be taller. And Ginny insisted on starting a pregnancy before he left, even though he'll be out of commo. Maybe, maybe a boy, a son—*stop it.* Think about anything. Bud. . . . Does Bud love Patty? Who knows? He loves Ginny. At seventy million miles. . . .

"Judy?" Luna Central or whoever it is says. "They don't answer. You want to try? But listen, we've been thinking. If these people really are from the past this must be very traumatic for them. They could be just realizing they'll never see their world again. Myda says these males had children and women they stayed with, they'll miss them terribly. This is exciting for us but it may seem awful to them. They could be too shocked to answer. They could be frightened, maybe they think we're aliens or hallucinations even. See?"

Five seconds later the nearby girl says, "Da, Margo, we were into that, too. Dinko. Ah, *Sunbird?* Major Davis of *Sunbird,* are you there? This is Judy Paris in the ship *Gloria,* we're only about a million kay from you, we see you on our screen." She sounds young and excited. "Luna Central has been trying to reach you, we think you're in trouble and we want to help. Please don't be frightened, we're people just like you. We think you're way off course if you want to reach Earth. Are you in trouble? Can we help? If your radio is out can you make any sort of signal? Do you know Old Morse? You'll be off our screen soon, we're truly worried about you. Please reply somehow if you possibly can, *Sunbird,* come in!"

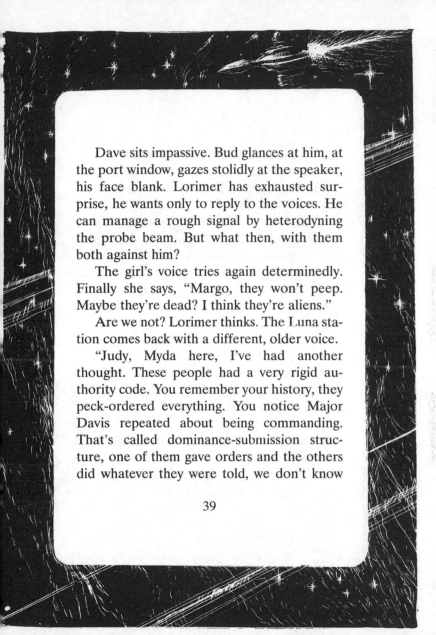

Dave sits impassive. Bud glances at him, at the port window, gazes stolidly at the speaker, his face blank. Lorimer has exhausted surprise, he wants only to reply to the voices. He can manage a rough signal by heterodyning the probe beam. But what then, with them both against him?

The girl's voice tries again determinedly. Finally she says, "Margo, they won't peep. Maybe they're dead? I think they're aliens."

Are we not? Lorimer thinks. The Luna station comes back with a different, older voice.

"Judy, Myda here, I've had another thought. These people had a very rigid authority code. You remember your history, they peck-ordered everything. You notice Major Davis repeated about being commanding. That's called dominance-submission structure, one of them gave orders and the others did whatever they were told, we don't know

39

quite why. Perhaps they were frightened. The point is that if the dominant one is in shock or panicked, maybe the others can't reply unless this Davis lets them."

Jesus Christ, Lorimer thinks. Jesus H. Christ in colors. It is his father's expression for the inexpressible. Dave and Bud sit unstirring.

"How weird," the Judy voice says. "But don't they know they're on a bad course? I mean, could the dominant one make the others fly right out of the system? Truly?"

It's happened, Lorimer thinks; it has happened. I have to stop this. I have to act now, before they lose us. Desperate visions of himself defying Dave and Bud loom before him. Try persuasion first.

Just as he opens his mouth he sees Bud stir slightly, and with immeasurable gratitude hears him say, "Dave-o, what say we take an eyeball look? One little old burp won't hurt us."

40

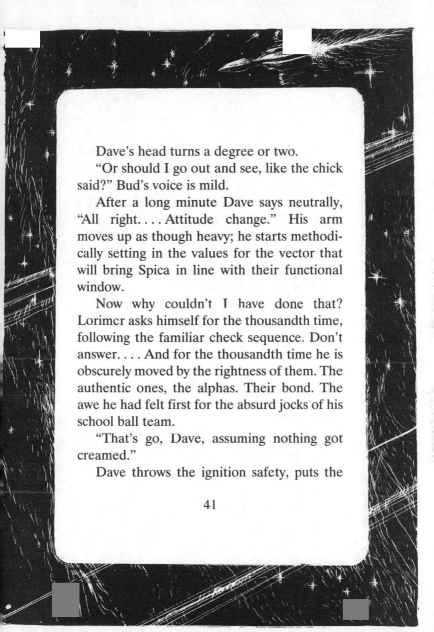

Dave's head turns a degree or two.

"Or should I go out and see, like the chick said?" Bud's voice is mild.

After a long minute Dave says neutrally, "All right.... Attitude change." His arm moves up as though heavy; he starts methodically setting in the values for the vector that will bring Spica in line with their functional window.

Now why couldn't I have done that? Lorimer asks himself for the thousandth time, following the familiar check sequence. Don't answer.... And for the thousandth time he is obscurely moved by the rightness of them. The authentic ones, the alphas. Their bond. The awe he had felt first for the absurd jocks of his school ball team.

"That's go, Dave, assuming nothing got creamed."

Dave throws the ignition safety, puts the

41

computer on real time. The hull shudders. Everything in the cabin drifts sidewise while the bright point of Spica swims the other way, appears on the front window as the retros cut in. When the star creeps out onto clear glass Lorimer can clearly see its companion. The double light steadies there; a beautiful job. He hands Bud the telescope.

"The one on the left."

Bud looks. "There she is, all right. Hey, Dave, look at that!"

He puts the scope in Dave's hand. Slowly, Dave raises it and looks. Lorimer can hear him breathe. Suddenly Dave pulls up the mike.

"Houston!" he says harshly. *"Sunbird* to Houston, *Sunbird* calling Houston. Houston, come in!"

Into the silence the speaker squeals, "They fired their engines—wait, she's calling!" And shuts up.

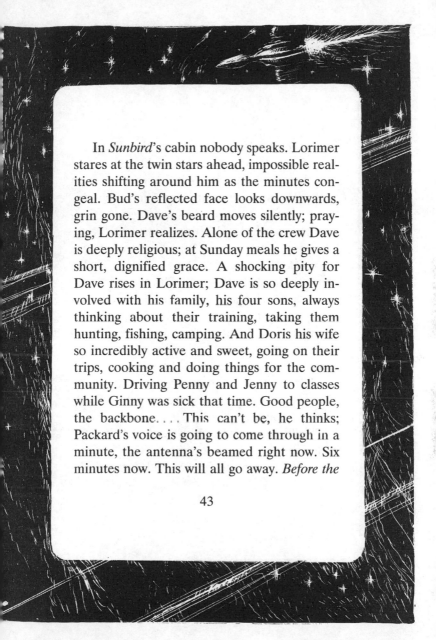

In *Sunbird*'s cabin nobody speaks. Lorimer stares at the twin stars ahead, impossible realities shifting around him as the minutes congeal. Bud's reflected face looks downwards, grin gone. Dave's beard moves silently; praying, Lorimer realizes. Alone of the crew Dave is deeply religious; at Sunday meals he gives a short, dignified grace. A shocking pity for Dave rises in Lorimer; Dave is so deeply involved with his family, his four sons, always thinking about their training, taking them hunting, fishing, camping. And Doris his wife so incredibly active and sweet, going on their trips, cooking and doing things for the community. Driving Penny and Jenny to classes while Ginny was sick that time. Good people, the backbone. . . . This can't be, he thinks; Packard's voice is going to come through in a minute, the antenna's beamed right now. Six minutes now. This will all go away. *Before the*

43

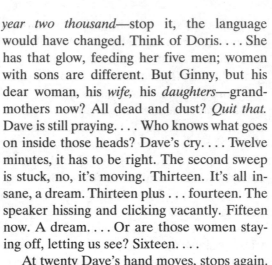

year two thousand—stop it, the language would have changed. Think of Doris. . . . She has that glow, feeding her five men; women with sons are different. But Ginny, but his dear woman, his *wife,* his *daughters*—grandmothers now? All dead and dust? *Quit that.* Dave is still praying. . . . Who knows what goes on inside those heads? Dave's cry. . . . Twelve minutes, it has to be right. The second sweep is stuck, no, it's moving. Thirteen. It's all insane, a dream. Thirteen plus . . . fourteen. The speaker hissing and clicking vacantly. Fifteen now. A dream. . . . Or are those women staying off, letting us see? Sixteen. . . .

At twenty Dave's hand moves, stops again. The seconds jitter by, space crackles. Thirty minutes coming up.

"Calling Major Davis in *Sunbird?*" It is the older woman, a gentle voice. "This is Luna Central. We are the service and communica-

44

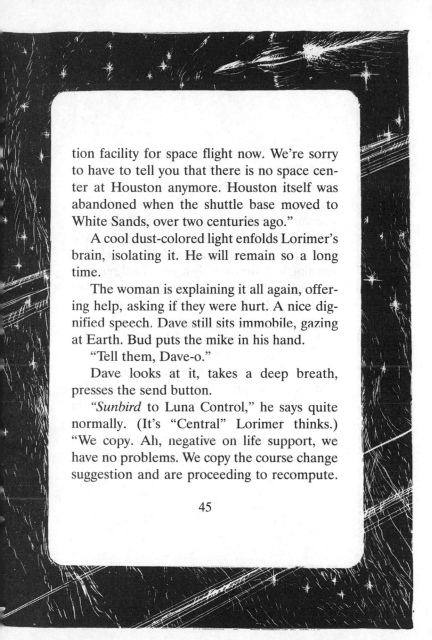

tion facility for space flight now. We're sorry to have to tell you that there is no space center at Houston anymore. Houston itself was abandoned when the shuttle base moved to White Sands, over two centuries ago."

A cool dust-colored light enfolds Lorimer's brain, isolating it. He will remain so a long time.

The woman is explaining it all again, offering help, asking if they were hurt. A nice dignified speech. Dave still sits immobile, gazing at Earth. Bud puts the mike in his hand.

"Tell them, Dave-o."

Dave looks at it, takes a deep breath, presses the send button.

"*Sunbird* to Luna Control," he says quite normally. (It's "Central" Lorimer thinks.) "We copy. Ah, negative on life support, we have no problems. We copy the course change suggestion and are proceeding to recompute.

45

Your offer of computer assistance is appreciated. We suggest you transmit position data so we can get squared away. Ah, we are economizing on transmission until we see how our accumulators have held up. *Sunbird* out."

And so it had begun.

Lorimer's mind floats back to himself now floating in *Gloria,* nearly a year, or three hundred years, later; watching and being watched by them. He still feels light, contented; the dread underneath has come no nearer. But it is so silent. He seems to have heard no voices for a long time. Or was it a long time? Maybe the drug is working on his time sense, maybe it was only a minute or two.

"I've been remembering," he says to the woman Connie, wanting her to speak.

She nods. "You have so much to remember. Oh, I'm sorry—that wasn't good to say." Her eyes speak sympathy.

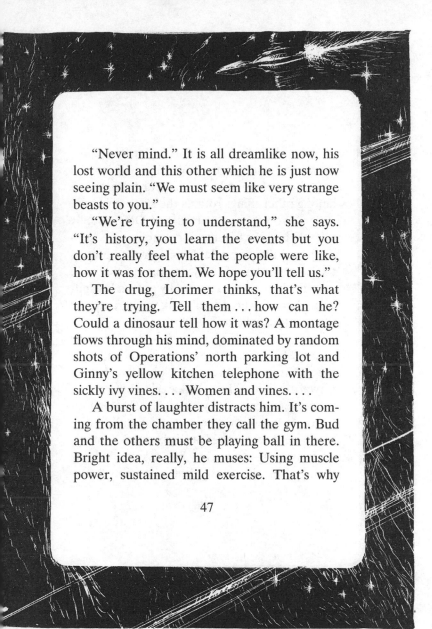

"Never mind." It is all dreamlike now, his lost world and this other which he is just now seeing plain. "We must seem like very strange beasts to you."

"We're trying to understand," she says. "It's history, you learn the events but you don't really feel what the people were like, how it was for them. We hope you'll tell us."

The drug, Lorimer thinks, that's what they're trying. Tell them . . . how can he? Could a dinosaur tell how it was? A montage flows through his mind, dominated by random shots of Operations' north parking lot and Ginny's yellow kitchen telephone with the sickly ivy vines. . . . Women and vines. . . .

A burst of laughter distracts him. It's coming from the chamber they call the gym. Bud and the others must be playing ball in there. Bright idea, really, he muses: Using muscle power, sustained mild exercise. That's why

47

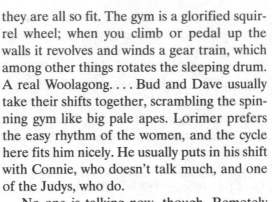

they are all so fit. The gym is a glorified squir-
rel wheel; when you climb or pedal up the
walls it revolves and winds a gear train, which
among other things rotates the sleeping drum.
A real Woolagong. . . . Bud and Dave usually
take their shifts together, scrambling the spinning gym like big pale apes. Lorimer prefers
the easy rhythm of the women, and the cycle
here fits him nicely. He usually puts in his shift
with Connie, who doesn't talk much, and one
of the Judys, who do.

No one is talking now, though. Remotely
uneasy, he looks around the big cylinder of
the cabin, sees Dave and Lady Blue by the
forward window. Judy Dakar is behind them,
silent for once. They must be looking at
Earth; it has been a beautiful expanding disk
for some weeks now. Dave's beard is moving,
he is praying again. He has taken to doing
that, not ostentatiously, but so obviously sin-

48

cere that Lorimer, a life atheist, can only sympathize.

The Judys have asked Dave what he whispers, of course. When Dave understood that they had no concept of prayer and had never seen a Christian Bible, there had been a heavy silence.

"So you have lost all faith," he said finally.

"We have faith," Judy Paris protested.

"May I ask in what?"

"We have faith in ourselves, of course," she told him.

"Young lady, if you were my daughter I'd tan your britches," Dave said, not joking. The subject was not raised again.

But he came back so well after that first dreadful shock, Lorimer thinks. A personal God, a father-model, man needs that. Dave draws strength from it and we lean on him. Maybe leaders have to believe. Dave was so

49

great; cheerful, unflappable, patiently working out alternatives, making his decisions on the inevitable discrepancies in the position readings in a way Lorimer couldn't do. A bitch. . . .

Memory takes him again; he is once again back in *Sunbird*, gritty-eyed, listening to the women's chatter, Dave's terse replies. God, how they chattered. But their computer work checks out. Lorimer is suffering also from a quirk of Dave's, his reluctance to transmit their exact thrust and fuel reserve. He keeps holding out a margin and making Lorimer compute it back in.

But the margins don't help; it is soon clear that they are in big trouble. Earth will pass too far ahead of them on her next orbit, they don't have the acceleration to catch up with her before they cross her path. They can carry out an ullage maneuver, they can kill enough velocity to let Earth catch them on the second go-by;

50

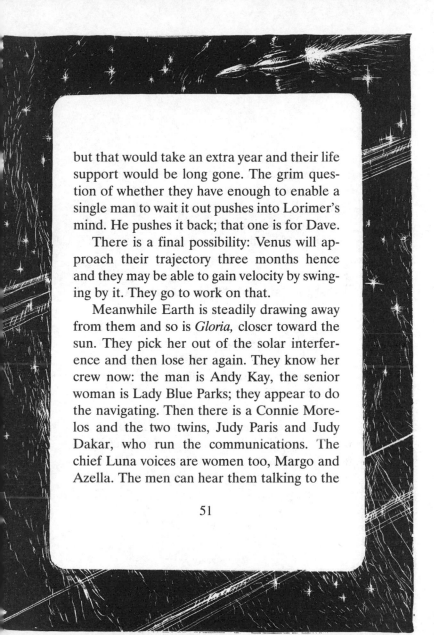

but that would take an extra year and their life support would be long gone. The grim question of whether they have enough to enable a single man to wait it out pushes into Lorimer's mind. He pushes it back; that one is for Dave.

There is a final possibility: Venus will approach their trajectory three months hence and they may be able to gain velocity by swinging by it. They go to work on that.

Meanwhile Earth is steadily drawing away from them and so is *Gloria,* closer toward the sun. They pick her out of the solar interference and then lose her again. They know her crew now: the man is Andy Kay, the senior woman is Lady Blue Parks; they appear to do the navigating. Then there is a Connie Morelos and the two twins, Judy Paris and Judy Dakar, who run the communications. The chief Luna voices are women too, Margo and Azella. The men can hear them talking to the

51

Escondita, which is now swinging in toward the far side of the sun. Dave insists on monitoring and taping everything that comes through. It proves to be largely replays of their exchanges with Luna and *Gloria,* mixed with a variety of highly personal messages. As references to cows, chickens, and other livestock multiply Dave reluctantly gives up his idea that they are code. Bud counts a total of five male voices.

"Big deal," he says. "There were more chick drivers on the road when we left. Means space is safe now, the girlies have taken over. Let them sweat their little asses off." He chuckles. "When we get this bird down, the stars ain't gonna study old Buddy no more, no, ma'am. A nice beach and about a zillion steaks and ale and all those sweet things. Hey, we'll be living history, we can charge admission."

Dave's face takes on the expression that

52

means an inappropriate topic has been breached. Much to Lorimer's impatience, Dave discourages all speculation as to what may await them on this future Earth. He confines their transmissions strictly to the problem in hand; when Lorimer tries to get him at least to mention the unchanged-language puzzle Dave only says firmly, "Later." Lorimer fumes; inconceivable that he is three centuries in the future, unable to learn a thing.

They do glcan a few facts from the women's talk. There have been nine successful *Sunbird* missions after theirs and one other casualty. And the *Gloria* and her sister ship are on a long-planned fly-by of the two inner planets.

"We always go along in pairs," Judy says. "But those planets are no good. Still, it was worth seeing."

"For Pete's sake, Dave, ask them how

53

many planets have been visited," Lorimer pleads.

"Later."

But about the fifth meal break Luna suddenly volunteers.

"Earth is making up a history for you, *Sunbird*," the Margo voice says. "We know you don't want to waste power asking, so we thought we'd send you a few main points right now." She laughs. "It's much harder than we thought, nobody here does history."

Lorimer nods to himself; he has been wondering what he could tell a man from 1690 who would want to know what happened to Cromwell—was Cromwell then?—and who had never heard of electricity, atoms, or the U.S.A.

"Let's see, probably the most important is that there aren't as many people as you had, we're just over two million. There was a world

54

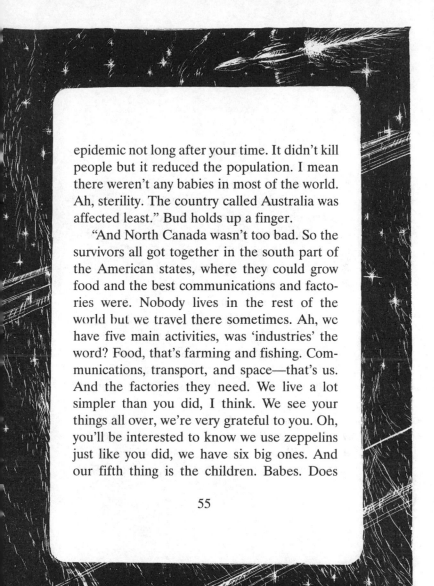

epidemic not long after your time. It didn't kill people but it reduced the population. I mean there weren't any babies in most of the world. Ah, sterility. The country called Australia was affected least." Bud holds up a finger.

"And North Canada wasn't too bad. So the survivors all got together in the south part of the American states, where they could grow food and the best communications and factories were. Nobody lives in the rest of the world but we travel there sometimes. Ah, we have five main activities, was 'industries' the word? Food, that's farming and fishing. Communications, transport, and space—that's us. And the factories they need. We live a lot simpler than you did, I think. We see your things all over, we're very grateful to you. Oh, you'll be interested to know we use zeppelins just like you did, we have six big ones. And our fifth thing is the children. Babes. Does that help? I'm using a children's book we have here."

The men have frozen during this recital; Lorimer is holding a cooling bag of hash. Bud starts chewing again and chokes.

"Two million people and a space capability?" He coughs. "That's incredible."

Dave gazes reflectively at the speaker. "There's a lot they're not telling us."

"I gotta ask them," Bud says. "Okay?"

Dave nods. "Watch it."

"Thanks for the history, Luna," Bud says. "We really appreciate it. But we can't figure out how you maintain a space program with only a couple of million people. Can you tell us a little more on that?"

In the pause Lorimer tries to grasp the staggering figures. From eight billion to two million . . . Europe, Asia, Africa, South America, America itself—wiped out. *There*

56

weren't any more babies. World sterility, from what? The Black Death, the famines of Asia—those had been decimations. This is magnitudes worse. No, it is all the same: beyond comprehension. An empty world, littered with junk.

"Sunbird?" says Margo. "Da, I should have thought you'd want to know about space. Well, we have only the four real spaceships and one building. You know the two here. Then there's *Indira* and *Pech,* they're on the Mars run now. Maybe the Mars dome was since your day. You had the satellite stations, though, didn't you? And the old Luna dome, of course—I remember now, it was during the epidemic. They tried to set up colonies to, ah, breed children, but the epidemic got there, too. They struggled terribly hard. We owe a lot to you really, you men I mean. The history has it all, how you worked out a minimal viable program

57

and trained everybody and saved it from the crazies. It was a glorious achievement. Oh, the marker here has one of your names on it. Lorimer. We love to keep it all going and growing, we all love traveling. Man is a rover, that's one of our mottoes."

"Are you hearing what I'm hearing?" Bud asks, blinking comically.

Dave is still staring at the speaker. "Not one word about their government," he says slowly. "Not a word about economic conditions. We're talking to a bunch of monkeys."

"Should I ask them?"

"Wait a minute . . . Roger, ask the name of their chief of state and the head of the space program. And—no, that's all."

"President?" Margo echoes Bud's query. "You mean like queens and kings? Wait, here's Myda. She's been talking about you with Earth."

The older woman they hear occasionally says *"Sunbird?* Da, we realize you had a very complex activity, your governments. With so few people we don't have that type of formal structure at all. People from the different activities meet periodically and our communications are good, everyone is kept informed. The people in each activity are in charge of doing it while they're there. We rotate, you see. Mostly in five-year hitches; for example, Margo here was on the zeppelins and I've been on several factories and farms and of course the, well, the education, we all do that. I believe that's one big difference from you. And of course we all work. And things are basically far more stable now, I gather. We change slowly. Does that answer you? Of course, you can always ask Registry, they keep track of us all. But we can't, ah, take you to our leader, if that's what you mean." She

59

laughs, a genuine, jolly sound. "That's one of our old jokes. I must say," she goes on seriously, "it's been a joy to us that we can understand you so well. We make a big effort not to let the language drift, it would be tragic to lose touch with the past."

Dave takes the mike. "Thank you, Luna. You've given us something to think about. *Sunbird* out."

"How much of that is for real, Doc?" Bud rubs his curly head. "They're giving us one of your science fiction stories."

"The real story will come later," says Dave. "Our job is to get there."

"That's a point that doesn't look too good."

By the end of the session it looks worse. No Venus trajectory is any good. Lorimer reruns all the computations; same result.

"There doesn't seem to be any solution to

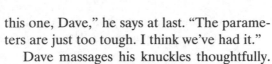

this one, Dave," he says at last. "The parameters are just too tough. I think we've had it."

Dave massages his knuckles thoughtfully. Then he nods. "Roger. We'll fire the optimum sequence on the Earth heading."

"Tell them to wave if they see us go by," says Bud.

They are silent, contemplating the prospect of a slow death in space eighteen months hence. Lorimer wonders if he can raise the other question, the bad one. He is pretty sure what Dave will say. What will he himself decide, what will he have the guts to do?

"Hello, *Sunbird?*" the voice of *Gloria* breaks in. "Listen, we've been figuring. We think if you use all your fuel you could come back in close enough to our orbit so we could swing out and pick you up. You'd be using solar gravity that way. We have plenty of maneuver but much less acceleration than you do.

61

You have suits and some kind of propellants, don't you? I mean, you could fly across a few kays?"

The three men look at each other; Lorimer guesses he had not been the only one to speculate on that.

"That's a good thought, *Gloria,*" Dave says. "Let's hear what Luna says."

"Why?" asks Judy. "It's our business, we wouldn't endanger the ship. We'd only miss another look at Venus, who cares? We have plenty of water and food and if the air gets a little smelly we can stand it."

"Hey, the chicks are all right," Bud says. They wait.

The voice of Luna comes on. "We've been looking at that, too, Judy. We're not sure you understand the risk. Ah, *Sunbird,* excuse me. Judy, if you manage to pick them up you'll have to spend nearly a year in the ship with

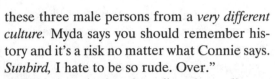

these three male persons from a *very different culture.* Myda says you should remember history and it's a risk no matter what Connie says. *Sunbird,* I hate to be so rude. Over."

Bud is grinning broadly, they all are. "Cavemen." He chuckles. "All the chicks land preggers."

"Margo, they're human beings," the Judy voice protests. "This isn't just Connie, we're all agreed. Andy and Lady Blue say it would be very interesting. If it works, that is. We can't let them go without trying."

"We feel that way, too, of course," Luna replies. "But there's another problem. They could be carrying diseases. *Sunbird,* I know you've been isolated for fourteen months, but Murti says people in your day were immune to organisms that aren't around now. Maybe some of ours could harm you, too. You could all get mortally sick and lose the ship."

63

"We thought of that, Margo," Judy says impatiently. "Look, if you have contact with them at all somebody has to test, true? So we're ideal. By the time we get home you'll know. And how could we get sick so fast we couldn't put *Gloria* in a stable orbit where you could get her later on?"

They wait. "Hey, what about that epidemic?" Bud pats his hair elaborately. "I don't know if I want a career in gay lib."

"You rather stay out here?" Dave asks.

"Crazies," says a different voice from Luna. *"Sunbird,* I'm Murti, the health person here. I think what we have to fear most is the meningitis-influenza complex, they mutate so readily. Does your Dr. Lorimer have any suggestions?"

"Roger, I'll put him on," says Dave. "But as to your first point, madam, I want to inform you that at the time of takeoff the incidence of

64

rape in the United States space cadre was zero point zero. I guarantee the conduct of my crew provided you can control yours. Here is Dr. Lorimer."

But Lorimer cannot, of course, tell them anything useful. They discuss the men's polio shots, which luckily have used killed virus, and various childhood diseases which still seem to be around. He does not mention their epidemic.

"Luna, we're going to try it," Judy declares. "We couldn't live with ourselves. Now, let's get the course figured before they get any farther away."

From there on, there is no rest on *Sunbird* while they set up and refigure and rerun the computations for the envelope of possible intersecting trajectories. The *Gloria*'s drive, they learn, is indeed low-thrust, although capable of sustained operation. *Sunbird* will have to get most of the way to the rendezvous on her own if they can cancel their outward velocity.

The tension breaks once during the long session, when Luna calls *Gloria* to warn Connie to be sure the female crew members wear concealing garments at all times if the men came aboard.

"Not suit liners, Connie, they're much too tight." It is the older woman, Myda. Bud chuckles.

"Your light sleepers, I think. And when the men unsuit, your Andy is the only one who should help them. You others stay away. The same for all body functions and sleeping. This is very important, Connie, you'll have to watch it the whole way home. There are a great many complicated taboos. I'm putting an instruction list on the bleeper. Is your receiver working?"

66

"Da, we used it for France's black hole paper."

"Good. Tell Judy to stand by. Now listen, Connie, listen carefully. Tell Andy he has to read it all. I repeat, *he* has to read every word. Did you hear that?"

"Ah, dinko," Connie answers. "I understand, Myda. He will."

"I think we just lost the ball game, fellas," Bud laments. "Old mother Myda took it all away."

Even Dave laughs. But later when the modulated squeal that is a whole text comes through the speaker, he frowns again. "There goes the good stuff."

The last factors are cranked in; the revised program spins, and Luna confirms them. "We have a payout, Dave," Lorimer reports. "It's tight but there are at least two viable options. Provided the main jets are fully functional."

67

"We're going EVA to check."

That is exhausting; they find a warp in the deflector housing of the port engines and spend four sweating hours trying to wrestle it back. It is only Lorimer's third sight of open space but he is soon too tired to care.

"Best we can do," Dave pants finally. "We'll have to compensate in the psychic mode."

"You can do it, Dave-o," says Bud. "Hey, I gotta change those suit radios, don't let me forget."

In the psychic mode . . . Lorimer surfaces back to his real self, cocooned in *Gloria*'s big cluttered cabin, seeing Connie's living face. It must be hours, how long has he been dreaming?

"About two minutes." Connie smiles.

"I was thinking of the first time I saw you."

"Oh yes. We'll never forget that, ever."

Nor will he . . . He lets it unroll again in his head. The interminable hours after the first long burn, which has sent *Sunbird* yawing so they all have to gulp nausea pills. Judy's breathless voice reading down their approach: "Oh, very good, four hundred thousand . . . Oh great, *Sunbird,* you're almost three, you're going to break a hundred for sure—" Dave has done it, the big one.

Lorimer's probe is useless in the yaw, it isn't until they stabilize enough for the final burst that they can see the strange blip bloom and vanish in the slot. Converging, hopefully, on a theoretical near-intersection point.

"Here goes everything."

The final burn changes the yaw into a sickening tumble with the star field looping past the glass. The pills are no more use and the fuel feed to the attitude jets goes sour. They are all vomiting before they manage to

69

hand-pump the last of the fuel and slow the tumble.

"That's it, *Gloria.* Come and get us. Lights on, Bud. Let's get those suits up."

Fighting nausea, they go through the laborious routine in the fouled cabin. Suddenly Judy's voice sings out, "We see you, *Sunbird!* We see your light! Can't you see us?"

"No time," Dave says. But Bud, half suited, points at the window. "Fellas, oh, hey, look at that."

Lorimer stares, thinks he sees a faint spark between the whirling stars before he has to retch.

"Father, we thank you," says Dave quietly. "All right, move it on, Doc. Packs."

The effort of getting themselves plus the propulsion units and a couple of cargo nets out of the rolling ship drives everything else out of mind. It isn't until they are floating linked together and stabilized by Dave's hand jet that Lorimer has time to look.

The sun blanks out their left. A few meters below them *Sunbird* tumbles empty, looking absurdly small. Ahead of them, infinitely far away, is a point too blurred and yellow to be a star. It creeps: *Gloria,* on her approach tangent.

"Can you start, *Sunbird?*" says Judy in their helmets. "We don't want to brake any more on account of our exhaust. We estimate fifty kay in an hour, we're coming out on a line."

"Roger. Give me your jet, Doc."

"Goodbye, *Sunbird,*" says Bud. "Plenty of lead, Dave-o."

Lorimer finds it restful in a childish way, being towed across the abyss tied to the two big men. He has total confidence in Dave, he never considers the possibility that they will miss, sail by and be lost. Does Dave feel con-

71

tempt? Lorimer wonders; that banked-up silence, is it partly contempt for those who can manipulate only symbols, who have no mastery of matter? . . . He concentrates on mastering his stomach.

It is a long, dark trip. *Sunbird* shrinks to a twinkling light, slowly accelerating on the spiral course that will end her ultimately in the sun with their precious records that are three hundred years obsolete. With, also, the packet of photos and letters that Lorimer has twice put in his suit pouch and twice taken out. Now and then he catches sight of *Gloria,* growing from a blur to an incomprehensible tangle of lighted crescents.

"Woo-ee, it's big," Bud says. "No wonder they can't accelerate, that thing is a flying trailer park. It'd break up."

"It's a spaceship. Got those nets tight, Doc?"

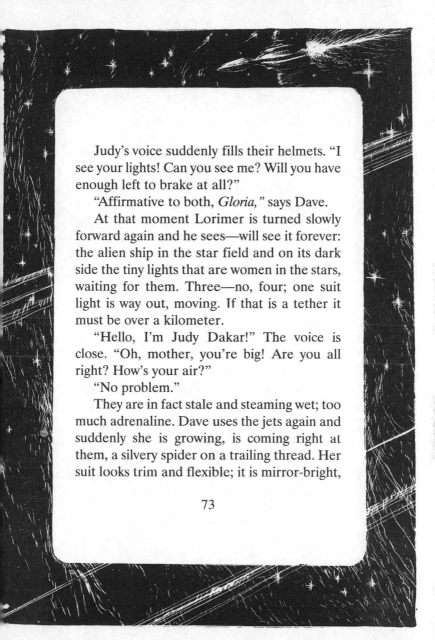

Judy's voice suddenly fills their helmets. "I see your lights! Can you see me? Will you have enough left to brake at all?"

"Affirmative to both, *Gloria,*" says Dave.

At that moment Lorimer is turned slowly forward again and he sees—will see it forever: the alien ship in the star field and on its dark side the tiny lights that are women in the stars, waiting for them. Three—no, four; one suit light is way out, moving. If that is a tether it must be over a kilometer.

"Hello, I'm Judy Dakar!" The voice is close. "Oh, mother, you're big! Are you all right? How's your air?"

"No problem."

They are in fact stale and steaming wet; too much adrenaline. Dave uses the jets again and suddenly she is growing, is coming right at them, a silvery spider on a trailing thread. Her suit looks trim and flexible; it is mirror-bright,

73

and the pack is quite small. Marvels of the future, Lorimer thinks; Paragraph One.

"You made it, you made it! Here, tie in. Brake!"

"There ought to be some historic words," Bud murmurs. "If she gives us a chance."

"Hello, Judy," says Dave calmly. "Thanks for coming."

"Contact!" She blasts their ears. "Haul us in, Andy! Brake, brake—the exhaust is back there!"

And they are grabbed hard, deflected into a great arc toward the ship. Dave uses up the last jet. The line loops.

"Don't jerk it," Judy cries. "Oh, I'm *sorry.*" She is clinging on them like a gibbon, Lorimer can see her eyes, her excited mouth. Incredible. "Watch out, it's slack."

"Teach me, honey," says Andy's baritone. Lorimer twists and sees him far back at the

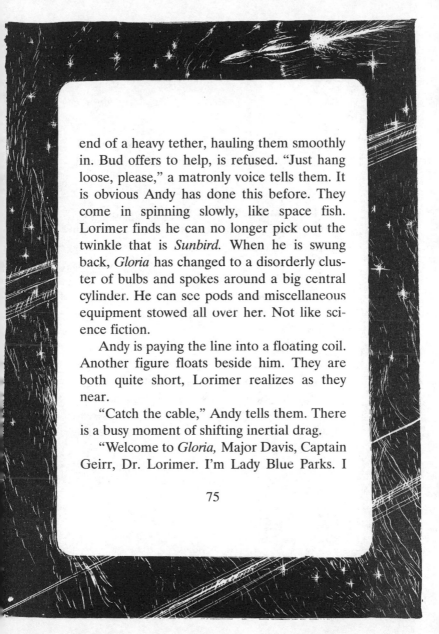

end of a heavy tether, hauling them smoothly in. Bud offers to help, is refused. "Just hang loose, please," a matronly voice tells them. It is obvious Andy has done this before. They come in spinning slowly, like space fish. Lorimer finds he can no longer pick out the twinkle that is *Sunbird.* When he is swung back, *Gloria* has changed to a disorderly cluster of bulbs and spokes around a big central cylinder. He can see pods and miscellaneous equipment stowed all over her. Not like science fiction.

Andy is paying the line into a floating coil. Another figure floats beside him. They are both quite short, Lorimer realizes as they near.

"Catch the cable," Andy tells them. There is a busy moment of shifting inertial drag.

"Welcome to *Gloria,* Major Davis, Captain Geirr, Dr. Lorimer. I'm Lady Blue Parks. I

75

think you'll like to get inside as soon as possible. If you feel like climbing go right ahead, we'll pull all this in later."

"We appreciate it, ma'am."

They start hand over hand along the catenary of the main tether. It has a good rough grip. Judy coasts up to peer at them, smiling broadly, towing the coil. A taller figure waits by the ship's open airlock.

"Hello, I'm Connie. I think we can cycle in two at a time. Will you come with me, Major Davis?"

It is like an emergency on a plane, Lorimer thinks as Dave follows her in. Being ordered about by supernaturally polite little girls.

"Space-going stews." Bud nudges him. "How 'bout that?" His face is sprouting sweat. Lorimer tells him to go next, his own LSP has less load.

Bud goes in with Andy. The woman named

76

Lady Blue waits beside Lorimer while Judy scrambles on the hull securing their cargo nets. She doesn't seem to have magnetic soles; perhaps ferrous metals aren't used in space now. When she begins hauling in the main tether on a simple hand winch Lady Blue looks at it critically.

"I used to make those," she says to Lorimer. What he can see of her features looks compressed, her dark eyes twinkle. He has the impression she is part black.

"I ought to get over and clean that aft antenna." Judy floats up. "Later," says Lady Blue. They both smile at Lorimer. Then the hatch opens and he and Lady Blue go in. When the toggles seat there comes a rising scream of air and Lorimer's suit collapses.

"Can I help you?" She has opened her faceplate, the voice is rich and live. Eagerly Lorimer catches the latches in his clumsy gloves and lets her lift the helmet off. His first breath surprises him, it takes an instant to identify the gas as fresh air. Then the inner hatch opens, letting in greenish light. She waves him through. He swims into a short tunnel. Voices are coming from around the corner ahead. His hand finds a grip and he stops, feeling his heart shudder in his chest.

When he turns that corner the world he knows will be dead. Gone, rolled up, blown away forever with *Sunbird*. He will be irrevocably in the future. A man from the past, a time traveler. In the future. . . .

He pulls himself around the bend.

The future is a vast bright cylinder, its whole inner surface festooned with unidentifiable objects, fronds of green. In front of him floats an odd tableau: Bud and Dave, helmets off, looking enormous in their bulky white suits and packs. A few meters away hang two bareheaded figures in shiny suits and a dark-haired girl in flowing pink pajamas.

They are all simply staring at the two men, their eyes and mouths open in identical expressions of pleased wonder. The face that has to be Andy's is grinning openmouthed like a kid at the zoo. He is a surprisingly young boy, Lorimer sees, in spite of his deep voice; blond, downy-cheeked, compactly muscular. Lorimer finds he can scarcely bear to look at the pink woman, can't tell if she really is surpassingly beautiful or plain. The taller suited woman has a shiny, ordinary face.

From overhead bursts an extraordinary sound which he finally recognizes as a chicken cackling. Lady Blue pushes past him.

"All right, Andy, Connie, stop staring and help them get their suits off. Judy, Luna is just as eager to hear about this as we are."

The tableau jumps to life. Afterwards

79

Lorimer can recall mostly eyes, bright curious eyes tugging his boots, smiling eyes upside down over his pack—and always that light, ready laughter. Andy is left alone to help them peel down, blinking at the fittings which Lorimer still finds embarrassing. He seems easy and nimble in his own half-open suit. Lorimer struggles out of the last lacings, thinking: A boy! A boy and four women orbiting the sun, flying their big junky ships to Mars. Should he feel humiliated? He only feels grateful, accepting a short robe and a bulb of tea somebody—Connie?—gives him.

The suited Judy comes in with their nets. The men follow Andy along another passage, Bud and Dave clutching at the small robes. Andy stops by a hatch.

"This greenhouse is for you, it's your toilet. Three's a lot but you have full sun."

Inside is a brilliant jungle, foliage everywhere, glittering water droplets, rustling leaves. Something whirs away—a grasshopper.

"You crank that handle." Andy points to a seat on a large cross-duct. "The piston rams the gravel and waste into a compost process and it ends up in the soil core. That vetch is a heavy nitrogen user and a great oxidator. We pump CO_2 in and oxy out. It's a real Woolagong."

He watches critically while Bud tries out the facility.

"What's a Woolagong?" asks Lorimer dazedly.

"Oh, she's one of our inventors. Some of her stuff is weird. When we have a pluggy-looking thing that works we call it a Woolagong." He grins. "The chickens eat the seeds and the hoppers, see, and the hoppers and iguanas eat the leaves. When a green-house is going darkside we turn them in to

81

harvest. With this much light I think we could keep a goat, don't you? You didn't have any life at all on your ship, true?"

"No," Lorimer says, "not a single iguana."

"They promised us a Shetland pony for Christmas," says Bud, rattling gravel. Andy joins perplexedly in the laugh.

Lorimer's head is foggy; it isn't only fatigue, the year in *Sunbird* has atrophied his ability to take in novelty. Numbly he uses the Woolagong and they go back out and forward to *Gloria*'s big control room, where Dave makes a neat short speech to Luna and is answered graciously.

"We have to finish changing course now," Lady Blue says. Lorimer's impression has been right, she is a small light part-Negro in late middle age. Connie is part something exotic, too, he sees; the others are European types.

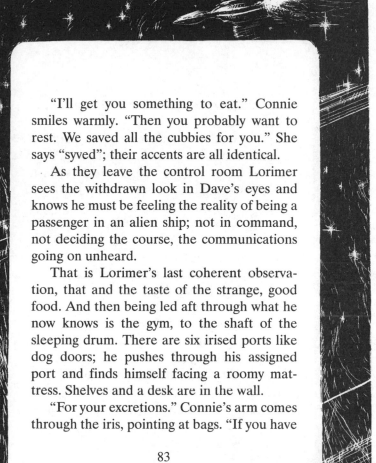

"I'll get you something to eat." Connie smiles warmly. "Then you probably want to rest. We saved all the cubbies for you." She says "syved"; their accents are all identical.

As they leave the control room Lorimer sees the withdrawn look in Dave's eyes and knows he must be feeling the reality of being a passenger in an alien ship; not in command, not deciding the course, the communications going on unheard.

That is Lorimer's last coherent observation, that and the taste of the strange, good food. And then being led aft through what he now knows is the gym, to the shaft of the sleeping drum. There are six irised ports like dog doors; he pushes through his assigned port and finds himself facing a roomy mattress. Shelves and a desk are in the wall.

"For your excretions." Connie's arm comes through the iris, pointing at bags. "If you have

83

a problem stick your head out and call. There's water."

Lorimer simply drifts toward the mattress, too sweated out to reply. His drifting ends in a curious heavy settling and his final astonishment: the drum is smoothly, silently starting to revolve. He sinks gratefully onto the pad, growing "heavier" as the minutes pass. About a tenth gee, maybe more, he thinks, it's still accelerating. And falls into the most restful sleep he has known in the long weary year.

It isn't till next day that he understands that Connie and two others have been on the rungs of the gym chamber, sending it around hour after hour without pause or effort and chatting as they went.

How they talk, he thinks, again floating back to real present time. The bubbling irritant pours through his memory, the voices of Ginny and Jenny and Penny on the kitchen

84

telephone, before that his mother's voice, his sister Amy's. Interminable. What do they always have to talk, talk, talk of?

"Why, everything," says the real voice of Connie beside him now, "it's natural to share."

"Natural. . . ." Like ants, he thinks. They twiddle their antennae together every time they meet. Where did you go, what did you do? Twiddle-twiddle. How do you *feel?* Oh, I feel this, I feel that, blah blah twiddle-twiddle. Total coordination of the hive. Women have no self-respect. Say anything, no sense of the strategy of words, the dark danger of naming. Can't hold in.

"Ants, beehives." Connie laughs, showing the bad tooth. "You truly see us as insects, don't you? Because they're females?"

"Was I talking aloud? I'm sorry." He blinks away dreams.

85

"Oh, please don't be. It's so sad to hear about your sister and your children and your, your wife. They must have been wonderful people. We think you're very brave."

But he has only thought of Ginny and them all for an instant—what has he been babbling? What is the drug doing to him?

"What are you doing to us?" he demands, lanced by real alarm now, almost angry.

"It's all right, truly." Her hand touches his, warm and somehow shy. "We all use it when we need to explore something. Usually it's pleasant. It's a laevonoramine compound, a disinhibitor, it doesn't dull you like alcohol. We'll be home so soon, you see. We have the responsibility to understand and you're so locked in." Her eyes melt at him. "You don't feel sick, do you? We have the antidote."

"No . . ." His alarm has already flowed away somewhere. Her explanation strikes him

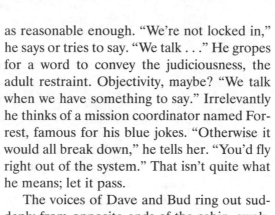

as reasonable enough. "We're not locked in," he says or tries to say. "We talk . . ." He gropes for a word to convey the judiciousness, the adult restraint. Objectivity, maybe? "We talk when we have something to say." Irrelevantly he thinks of a mission coordinator named Forrest, famous for his blue jokes. "Otherwise it would all break down," he tells her. "You'd fly right out of the system." That isn't quite what he means; let it pass.

The voices of Dave and Bud ring out suddenly from opposite ends of the cabin, awakening the foreboding of evil in his mind. They don't know us, he thinks. They should look out, stop this. But he is feeling too serene, he wants to think about his own new understanding, the pattern of them all he is seeing at last.

"I feel lucid," he manages to say, "I want to think."

She looks pleased. "We call that the

ataraxia effect. It's so nice when it goes that way."

Ataraxia, philosophical calm. Yes. But there are monsters in the deep, he thinks or says. The night side. The night side of Orren Lorimer, a self hotly dark and complex, waiting in leash. They're so vulnerable. They don't know we can take them. Images rush up: a Judy spread-eagled on the gym rungs, pink pajamas gone, open to him. Flash sequence of the three of them taking over the ship, the women tied up, helpless, shrieking, raped and used. The team—get the satellite station, get a shuttle down to Earth. Hostages. Make them do anything, no defense whatever . . . Has Bud actually said that? But Bud doesn't know, he remembers. Dave knows they're hiding something, but he thinks it's socialism or sin. When they find out . . .

How has he himself found out? Simply listening, really, all these months. He listens to their talk much more than the others; "fraternizing," Dave calls it. . . . They all listened at first, of course. Listened and looked and reacted helplessly to the female bodies, the tender bulges so close under the thin, tantalizing clothes, the magnetic mouths and eyes, the smell of them, their electric touch. Watching them touch each other, touch Andy, laughing, vanishing quietly into shared bunks. *What goes on? Can I? My need, my need—*

The power of them, the fierce resentment. . . . Bud muttered and groaned meaningfully despite Dave's warnings. He kept needling Andy until Dave banned all questions. Dave himself was noticeably tense and read his Bible a great deal. Lorimer found his own body pointing after them like a famished hound, hoping to Christ the cubicles are as they appeared to be, unwired.

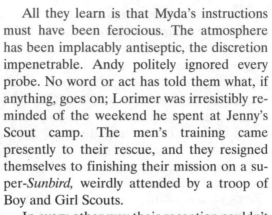

All they learn is that Myda's instructions must have been ferocious. The atmosphere has been implacably antiseptic, the discretion impenetrable. Andy politely ignored every probe. No word or act has told them what, if anything, goes on; Lorimer was irresistibly reminded of the weekend he spent at Jenny's Scout camp. The men's training came presently to their rescue, and they resigned themselves to finishing their mission on a super-*Sunbird,* weirdly attended by a troop of Boy and Girl Scouts.

In every other way their reception couldn't be more courteous. They have been given the run of the ship and their own dayroom in a cleaned-out gravel storage pod. They visit the control room as they wish. Lady Blue and Andy give them specs and manuals and show them every circuit and device of *Gloria,* inside and out. Luna has bleeped up a stream of sci-

90

ence texts and the data on all their satellites and shuttles and the Mars and Luna dome colonies.

Dave and Bud plunged into an orgy of engineering. *Gloria* is, as they suspected, powered by a fission plant that uses a range of Lunar materials. Her ion drive is only slightly advanced over the experimental models of their own day. The marvels of the future seem so far to consist mainly of ingenious modifications.

"It's primitive," Bud tells him. "What they've done is sacrifice everything to keep it simple and easy to maintain. Believe it, they can hand-feed fuel. And the backups, brother! They have redundant redundancy."

But Lorimer's technical interest soon flags. What he really wants is to be alone a while. He makes a desultory attempt to survey the apparently few developments in his

91

field, and finds he can't concentrate. What the hell, he tells himself, I stopped being a physicist three hundred years ago. Such a relief to be out of the cell of *Sunbird;* he has given himself up to drifting solitary through the warren of the ship, using their excellent 400 mm telescope, noting the odd life of the crew.

When he finds that Lady Blue likes chess they form a routine of biweekly games. Her personality intrigues him; she has reserve and an aura of authority. But she quickly stops Bud when he calls her "Captain."

"No one here commands in your sense. I'm just the oldest." Bud goes back to "ma'am."

She plays a solid positional game, somewhat more erratic than a man but with occasional elegant traps. Lorimer is astonished to find that there is only one new chess opening, an interesting queen-side gambit called the

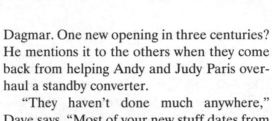

Dagmar. One new opening in three centuries?
He mentions it to the others when they come
back from helping Andy and Judy Paris over-
haul a standby converter.

"They haven't done much anywhere,"
Dave says. "Most of your new stuff dates from
the epidemic, Andy, if you'll pardon me. The
program seems to be stagnating. You've been
gearing up this Titan project for eighty years."

"We'll get there." Andy grins.

"C'mon, Dave," says Bud. "Judy and me
are taking on you two for the next chicken dinner, we'll get a bridge team here yet. Woo-ee,
I can taste that chicken! Losers get the
iguana."

The food is so good. Lorimer finds himself
lingering around the kitchen end, helping
whoever is cooking, munching on their various
seeds and chewy roots as he listens to them
talk. He even likes the iguana. He begins to

93

put on weight, in fact they all do. Dave decrees double exercise shifts.

"You going to make us *climb* home, Dave-o?" Bud groans. But Lorimer enjoys it, pedaling or swinging easily along the rungs while the women chat and listen to tapes. Familiar music: he identifies a strange spectrum from Handel, Brahms, Sibelius, through Strauss to ballad tunes and intricate light jazz rock. No lyrics. But plenty of informative texts doubtless selected for his benefit.

From the promised short history he finds out more about the epidemic. It seems to have been an airborne quasi-virus escaped from Franco-Arab military labs, possibly potentiated by pollutants.

"It apparently damaged only the reproductive cells," he tells Dave and Bud. "There was little actual mortality, but almost universal sterility. Probably a molecular substitution in

94

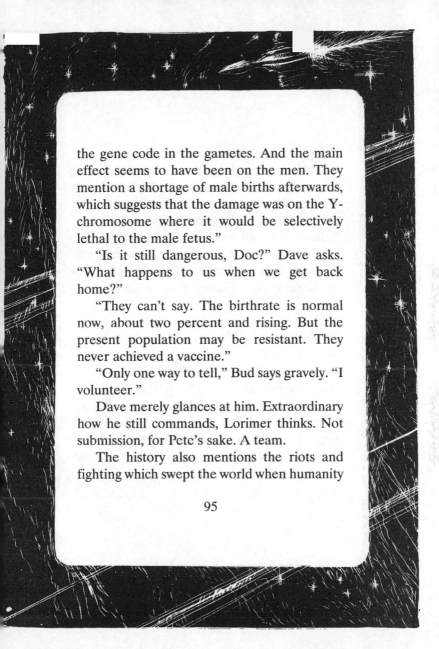

the gene code in the gametes. And the main
effect seems to have been on the men. They
mention a shortage of male births afterwards,
which suggests that the damage was on the Y-
chromosome where it would be selectively
lethal to the male fetus."

"Is it still dangerous, Doc?" Dave asks.
"What happens to us when we get back
home?"

"They can't say. The birthrate is normal
now, about two percent and rising. But the
present population may be resistant. They
never achieved a vaccine."

"Only one way to tell," Bud says gravely. "I
volunteer."

Dave merely glances at him. Extraordinary
how he still commands, Lorimer thinks. Not
submission, for Pctc's sake. A team.

The history also mentions the riots and
fighting which swept the world when humanity

95

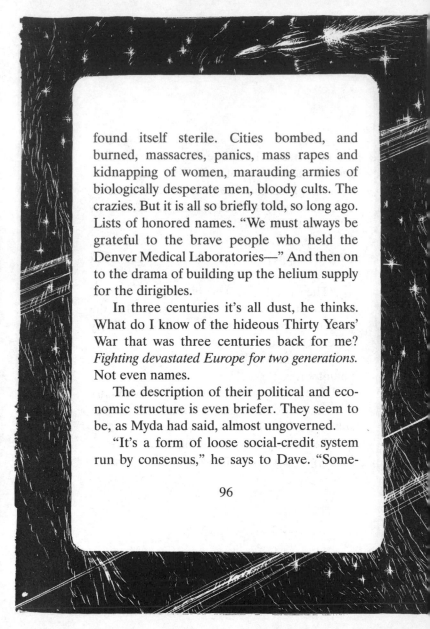

found itself sterile. Cities bombed, and burned, massacres, panics, mass rapes and kidnapping of women, marauding armies of biologically desperate men, bloody cults. The crazies. But it is all so briefly told, so long ago. Lists of honored names. "We must always be grateful to the brave people who held the Denver Medical Laboratories—" And then on to the drama of building up the helium supply for the dirigibles.

In three centuries it's all dust, he thinks. What do I know of the hideous Thirty Years' War that was three centuries back for me? *Fighting devastated Europe for two generations.* Not even names.

The description of their political and economic structure is even briefer. They seem to be, as Myda had said, almost ungoverned.

"It's a form of loose social-credit system run by consensus," he says to Dave. "Some-

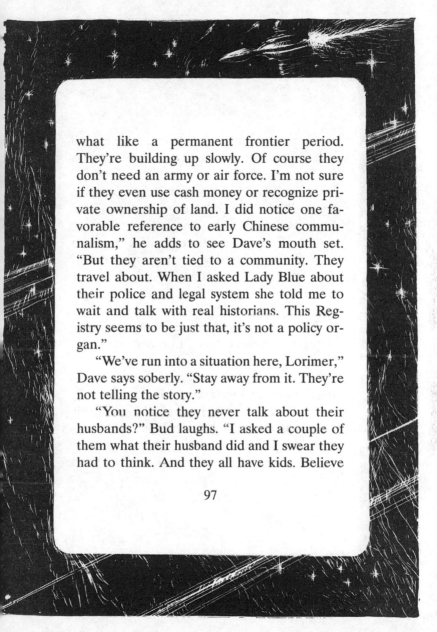

what like a permanent frontier period. They're building up slowly. Of course they don't need an army or air force. I'm not sure if they even use cash money or recognize private ownership of land. I did notice one favorable reference to early Chinese communalism," he adds to see Dave's mouth set. "But they aren't tied to a community. They travel about. When I asked Lady Blue about their police and legal system she told me to wait and talk with real historians. This Registry seems to be just that, it's not a policy organ."

"We've run into a situation here, Lorimer," Dave says soberly. "Stay away from it. They're not telling the story."

"You notice they never talk about their husbands?" Bud laughs. "I asked a couple of them what their husband did and I swear they had to think. And they all have kids. Believe

97

me, it's a swinging scene down there, even if old Andy acts like he hasn't found out what it's for."

"I don't want any prying into their personal family lives while we're on this ship, Geirr. None whatsoever. That's an order."

"Maybe they don't have families. You ever hear 'em mention anybody getting married? That has to be the one thing on a chick's mind. Mark my words, there's been some changes made."

"The social mores are bound to have changed to some extent," Lorimer says. "Obviously you have women doing more work outside the home, for one thing. But they have family bonds; for instance, Lady Blue has a sister in an aluminum mill and another in health. Andy's mother is on Mars and his sister works in Registry. Connie has a brother or brothers on the fishing fleet near Biloxi, and her sister is coming out to replace her here next trip, she's making yeast now."

"That's the top of the iceberg."

"I doubt the rest of the iceberg is very sinister, Dave."

But somewhere along the line the blandness begins to bother Lorimer, too. So much is missing. Marriage, love affairs, children's troubles, jealousy squabbles, status, possessions, money problems, sicknesses, funerals even—all the daily minutiae that occupied Ginny and her friend seems to have been edited out of these women's talk. *Edited.* . . . Can Dave be right? Is some big, significant aspect being deliberately kept from them?

"I'm still surprised your language hasn't changed more," he says one day to Connie during their exertions in the gym.

"Oh, we're very careful about that." She climbs at an angle beside him, not using her hands. "It would be a dreadful loss if we couldn't understand the books. All the children are taught from the same original tapes, you see. Oh, there's faddy words we use for a while, but our communicators have to learn the old texts by heart, that keeps us together."

Judy Paris grunts from the pedicycle. "You, my dear children, will never know the oppression we suffered," she declaims mockingly.

"Judys talk too much," says Connie.

"We do, for a fact." They both laugh.

"So you still read our so-called great books, our fiction and poetry?" asks Lorimer. "Who do you read, H. G. Wells? Shakespeare? Dickens, ah, Balzac, Kipling, Brian?" He gropes; Brian had been a bestseller Ginny liked. When had he last looked at Shakespeare or the others?

"Oh, the historicals," Judy says. "It's interesting, I guess. Grim. They're not very realistic. I'm sure it was to you," she adds generously.

And they turn to discussing whether the laying hens are getting too much light, leaving Lorimer to wonder how what he supposes are the eternal verities of human nature can have faded from a world's reality. Love, conflict, heroism, tragedy—all "unrealistic"? Well, flight crews are never great readers; still, women read more.... Something *has* changed, he can sense it. Something basic enough to affect human nature. A physical development perhaps; a mutation? What is really under those floating clothes?

It is the Judys who give him part of it.

He is exercising alone with both of them, listening to them gossip about some legendary figure named Dagmar.

"The Dagmar who invented the chess opening?" he asks.

"Yes. She does anything, when she's good she's great."

"Was she bad sometimes?"

A Judy laughs. "The Dagmar problem, you can say. She has this tendency to organize everything. It's fine when it works but every so often it runs wild, she thinks she's queen or what. Then they have to get out the butterfly nets."

All in present tense—but Lady Blue has told him the Dagmar gambit is over a century old.

Longevity, he thinks; by God, that's what they're hiding. Say they've achieved a doubled or tripled life span, that would certainly change human psychology, affect their outlook on everything. Delayed maturity, perhaps? We were working on endocrine cell juvenescence when I left. How old are these girls, for instance?

102

He is framing a question when Judy Dakar says, "I was in the crèche when she went pluggo. But she's good, I loved her later on."

Lorimer thinks she has said "crash" and then realizes she means a communal nursery. "Is that the same Dagmar?" he asks. "She must be very old."

"Oh no, her sister."

"A sister a hundred years apart?"

"I mean, her daughter. Her, her *grand*-daughter." She starts pedaling fast.

"Judy," says her twin, behind them.

Sister again. Everybody he learns of seems to have an extraordinary number of sisters, Lorimer reflects. He hears Judy Paris saying to her twin, "I think I remember Dagmar at the crèche. She started uniforms for everybody. Colors and numbers."

"You couldn't have, you weren't born," Judy Dakar retorts.

There is a silence in the drum.

Lorimer turns on the rungs to look at them. Two flushed cheerful faces stare back warily, make identical head-dipping gestures to swing the black hair out of their eyes. Identical. . . . But isn't the Dakar girl on the cycle a shade more mature, her face more weathered?

"I thought you were supposed to be twins."

"Ah, Judys talk a lot," they say together—and grin guiltily.

"You aren't sisters," he tells them. "You're what we called clones."

Another silence.

"Well, yes," says Judy Dakar. "We call it sisters. Oh, mother! We weren't supposed to tell you, Myda said you would be frightfully upset. It was illegal in your day, true?"

"Yes. We considered it immoral and unethical, experimenting with human life. But it doesn't upset me personally."

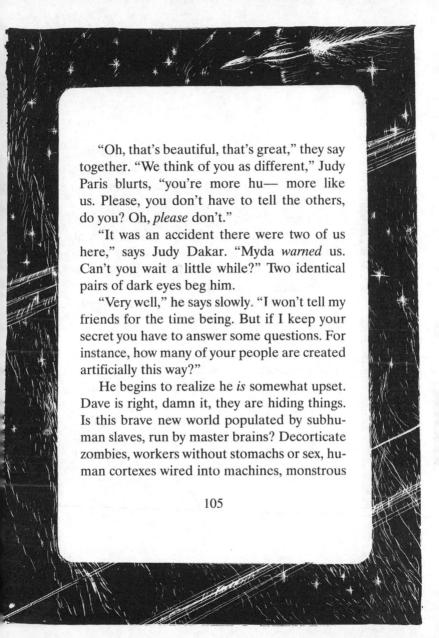

"Oh, that's beautiful, that's great," they say together. "We think of you as different," Judy Paris blurts, "you're more hu— more like us. Please, you don't have to tell the others, do you? Oh, *please* don't."

"It was an accident there were two of us here," says Judy Dakar. "Myda *warned* us. Can't you wait a little while?" Two identical pairs of dark eyes beg him.

"Very well," he says slowly. "I won't tell my friends for the time being. But if I keep your secret you have to answer some questions. For instance, how many of your people are created artificially this way?"

He begins to realize he *is* somewhat upset. Dave is right, damn it, they are hiding things. Is this brave new world populated by subhuman slaves, run by master brains? Decorticate zombies, workers without stomachs or sex, human cortexes wired into machines, monstrous

105

experiments rush through his mind. He had been naïve again. These normal-looking women can be fronting for a hideous world.

"How many?"

"There's only about eleven thousand of us," Judy Dakar says. The two Judys look at each other, transparently confirming something. They're unschooled in deception, Lorimer thinks; is that good? And is diverted by Judy Paris exclaiming, "What we can't figure out is why did you think it was wrong?"

Lorimer tries to tell them, to convey the horror of manipulating human identity, creating abnormal life. The threat to individuality, the fearful power it would put in a dictator's hand.

"Dictator?" one of them echoes blankly. He looks at their faces and can only say, "Doing things to people without their consent. I think it's sad."

"But that's just what we think about you," the younger Judy bursts out. "How do you know who you *are?* Or who anybody is? All alone, no sisters to share with! You don't know what you can do, or what would be interesting to try. All you poor singletons, you—why, you just have to blunder along and die, all for nothing!"

Her voice trembles. Amazed, Lorimer sees both of them are misty-eyed.

"We better get this m-moving," the other Judy says.

They swing back into the rhythm and in bits and pieces Lorimer finds out how it is. Not bottled embryos, they tell him indignantly. Human mothers like everybody else, young mothers, the best kind. A somatic cell nucleus is inserted in an enucleated ovum and reimplanted in the womb. They have each borne two "sister" babies in their late

107

teens and nursed them a while before moving on. The crèches always have plenty of mothers.

His longevity notion is laughed at; nothing but some rules of healthy living have as yet been achieved. "We should make ninety in good shape," they assure him. "A hundred and eight, that was Judy Eagle, she's our record. But she was pretty blah at the end."

The clone strains themselves are old, they date from the epidemic. They were part of the first effort to save the race when the babies stopped and they've continued ever since.

"It's so perfect," they tell him. "We each have a book, it's really a library. All the recorded messages. The Book of Judy Shapiro, that's us. Dakar and Paris are our personal names, we're doing cities now." They laugh, trying not to talk at once about how each Judy adds her individual memoir, her adventures and problems and discoveries in the genotype they all share.

"If you make a mistake it's useful for the others. Of course you try not to—or at least make a *new* one."

"Some of the old ones aren't so realistic," her other self puts in. "Things were so different, I guess. We make excerpts of the parts we like best. And practical things, like Judys should watch out for skin cancer."

"But we have to read the whole thing every ten years," says the Judy called Dakar. "It's inspiring. As you get older you understand some of the ones you didn't before."

Bemused, Lorimer tries to think how it would be, hearing the voices of three hundred years of Orren Lorimers. Lorimers who were mathematicians or plumbers or artists or bums or criminals, maybe. The continuing exploration and completion of self. And a dozen living doubles; aged Lorimers, infant Lorimers. And other Lorimers' women and children . . . would he enjoy it or resent it? He doesn't know.

"Have you made your records yet?"

"Oh, we're too young. Just notes in case of accident."

"Will we be in them?"

"You can say!" They laugh merrily, then sober. "Truly you won't tell?" Judy Paris asks. "Lady Blue, we have to let her know what we did. Oof. But *truly* you won't tell your friends?"

He hadn't told on them, he thinks now, emerging back into his living self. Connie beside him is drinking cider from a bulb. He has a drink in his hand, too, he finds. But he hasn't told.

"Judys will talk." Connie shakes her head, smiling. Lorimer realizes he must have gabbled out the whole thing.

110

"It doesn't matter," he tells her. "I would have guessed soon anyhow. There were too many clues ... Woolagongs invent, Mydas worry, Jans are brains, Billy Dees work so hard. I picked up six different stories of hydroelectric stations that were built or improved or are being run by one Lala Singh. Your whole way of life. I'm more interested in this sort of thing than a respectable physicist should be," he says wryly. "You're all clones, aren't you? Every one of you. What do Connies do?"

"You really do know." She gazes at him like a mother whose child has done something troublesome and bright. "Whew! Oh, well, Connies farm like mad, we grow things. Most of our names are plants. I'm Veronica, by the way. And of course the crèches, that's our weakness. The runt mania. We tend to focus on anything smaller or weak."

111

Her warm eyes focus on Lorimer, who draws back involuntarily.

"We control it." She gives a hearty chuckle. "We aren't all that way. There's been engineering Connies, and we have two young sisters who love metallurgy. It's fascinating what the genotype can do if you try. The original Constantia Morelos was a chemist, she weighed ninety pounds and never saw a farm in her life." Connie looks down at her own muscular arms. "She was killed by the crazies, she fought with weapons. It's so hard to understand . . . And I had a sister Timothy who made dynamite and dug two canals and she wasn't even an andy."

"An andy," he says.

"Oh, dear."

"I guessed that, too. Early androgen treatments."

She nods hesitantly. "Yes. We need the

112

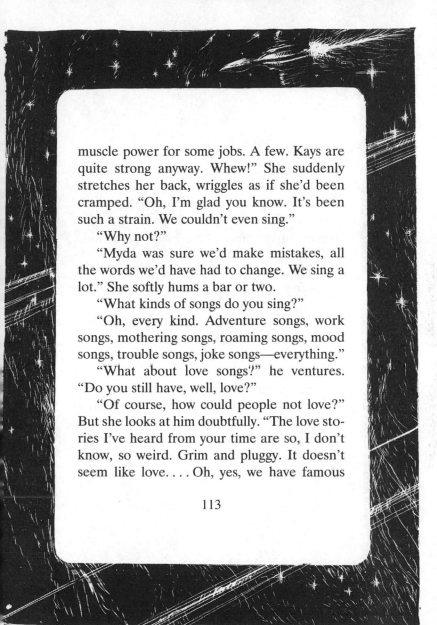

muscle power for some jobs. A few. Kays are quite strong anyway. Whew!" She suddenly stretches her back, wriggles as if she'd been cramped. "Oh, I'm glad you know. It's been such a strain. We couldn't even sing."

"Why not?"

"Myda was sure we'd make mistakes, all the words we'd have had to change. We sing a lot." She softly hums a bar or two.

"What kinds of songs do you sing?"

"Oh, every kind. Adventure songs, work songs, mothering songs, roaming songs, mood songs, trouble songs, joke songs—everything."

"What about love songs?" he ventures. "Do you still have, well, love?"

"Of course, how could people not love?" But she looks at him doubtfully. "The love stories I've heard from your time are so, I don't know, so weird. Grim and pluggy. It doesn't seem like love.... Oh, yes, we have famous

113

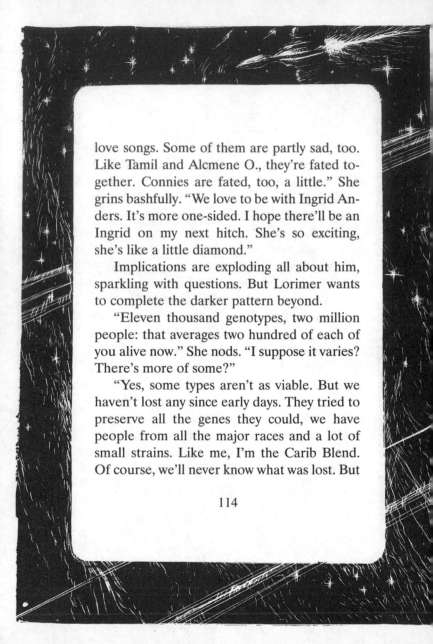

love songs. Some of them are partly sad, too. Like Tamil and Alcmene O., they're fated together. Connies are fated, too, a little." She grins bashfully. "We love to be with Ingrid Anders. It's more one-sided. I hope there'll be an Ingrid on my next hitch. She's so exciting, she's like a little diamond."

Implications are exploding all about him, sparkling with questions. But Lorimer wants to complete the darker pattern beyond.

"Eleven thousand genotypes, two million people: that averages two hundred of each of you alive now." She nods. "I suppose it varies? There's more of some?"

"Yes, some types aren't as viable. But we haven't lost any since early days. They tried to preserve all the genes they could, we have people from all the major races and a lot of small strains. Like me, I'm the Carib Blend. Of course, we'll never know what was lost. But

114

eleven thousand is a lot, really. We all try to know everyone, it's a life hobby."

A chill penetrates his ataraxia. Eleven thousand, period. That is the true population of Earth now. He thinks of two hundred tall olive-skinned women named after plants, excited by two hundred little bright Ingrids; two hundred talkative Judys, two hundred self-possessed Lady Blues, two hundred Margos and Mydas and the rest. He shivers. The heirs, the happy pallbearers of the human race.

"So evolution ends," he says somberly.

"No, why? It's just slowed down. We do everything much slower than you did, I think. We like to experience things *fully*. We have time." She stretches again, smiling. "There's all the time."

"But you have no new genotypes. It is the end."

115

"Oh but there are, now. Last century they worked out the way to make haploid nuclei combine. We can make a stripped egg cell function like pollen," she says proudly. "I mean sperm. It's tricky, some don't come out too well. But now we're finding both X's viable we have over a hundred new types started. Of course it's hard for them, with no sisters. The donors try to help."

Over a hundred, he thinks. Well. Maybe. ... But "both X's viable," what does that mean? She must be referring to the epidemic. But he had figured it primarily affected the men. His mind goes happily to work on the new puzzle, ignoring a sound from somewhere that is trying to pierce his calm.

"It was a gene or genes on the X chromosome that was injured," he guesses aloud. "Not the Y. And the lethal trait had to be recessive, right? Thus there would have been no

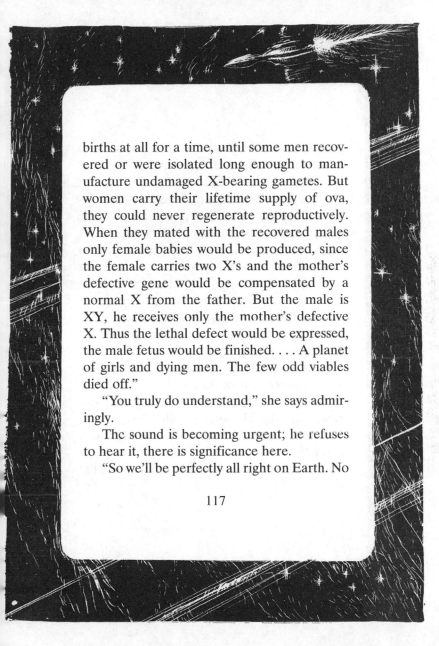

births at all for a time, until some men recovered or were isolated long enough to manufacture undamaged X-bearing gametes. But women carry their lifetime supply of ova, they could never regenerate reproductively. When they mated with the recovered males only female babies would be produced, since the female carries two X's and the mother's defective gene would be compensated by a normal X from the father. But the male is XY, he receives only the mother's defective X. Thus the lethal defect would be expressed, the male fetus would be finished. . . . A planet of girls and dying men. The few odd viables died off."

"You truly do understand," she says admiringly.

The sound is becoming urgent; he refuses to hear it, there is significance here.

"So we'll be perfectly all right on Earth. No

117

problem. In theory we can marry again and have families, daughters anyway."

"Yes," she says. "In theory."

The sound suddenly broaches his defenses, becomes the loud voice of Bud Geirr raised in song. He sounds plain drunk now. It seems to be coming from the main garden pod, the one they use to grow vegetables, not sanitation. Lorimer feels the dread alive again, rising closer. Dave ought to keep an eye on him. But Dave seems to have vanished, too, he recalls seeing him go toward Control with Lady Blue.

"OH, THE SUN SHINES BRIGHT ON PRET-TY RED WI-I-ING," carols Bud.

Something should be done, Lorimer decides painfully. He stirs; it is an effort.

"Don't worry," Connie says. "Andy's with them."

"You don't know, you don't know what

118

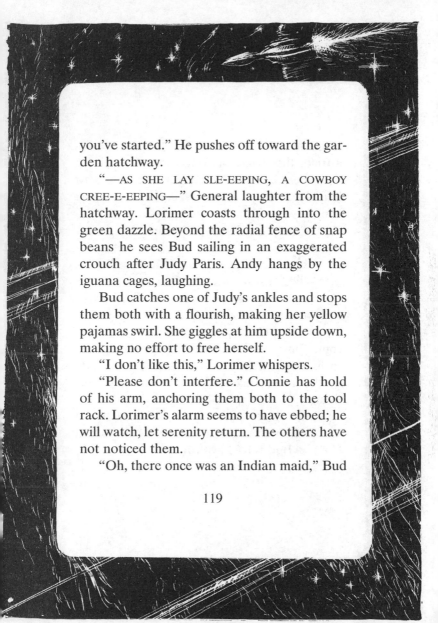

you've started." He pushes off toward the garden hatchway.

"—AS SHE LAY SLE-EEPING, A COWBOY CREE-E-EEPING—" General laughter from the hatchway. Lorimer coasts through into the green dazzle. Beyond the radial fence of snap beans he sees Bud sailing in an exaggerated crouch after Judy Paris. Andy hangs by the iguana cages, laughing.

Bud catches one of Judy's ankles and stops them both with a flourish, making her yellow pajamas swirl. She giggles at him upside down, making no effort to free herself.

"I don't like this," Lorimer whispers.

"Please don't interfere." Connie has hold of his arm, anchoring them both to the tool rack. Lorimer's alarm seems to have ebbed; he will watch, let serenity return. The others have not noticed them.

"Oh, there once was an Indian maid," Bud

119

sings more restrainedly, "who never was a-fraid, that some buckaroo would slip it up her, ahem, ahem." He coughs ostentatiously, laughing. "Hey, Andy, I hear them calling you."

"What?" says Judy. "I don't hear anything."

"They're calling you, lad. Out there."

"Who?" asks Andy, listening.

"*They* are, for Crissake." He lets go of Judy and kicks over to Andy. "Listen, you're a great kid. Can't you see me and Judy have some business to discuss in private?" He turns Andy gently around and pushes him at the bean stakes. "It's New Year's Eve, dummy."

Andy floats passively away through the fence of vines, raising a hand at Lorimer and Connie. Bud is back with Judy.

"Happy New Year, kitten." He smiles.

120

"Happy New Year. Did you do special things on New Year?" she asks curiously.

"What we did on New Year's." He chuckles, taking her shoulders in his hands. "On New Year's Eve, yes we did. Why don't I show you some of our primitive Earth customs, h'mm?"

She nods, wide-eyed.

"Well, first we wish each other well, like this." He draws her to him and lightly kisses her cheek. "Kee-rist, what a dumb bitch," he says in a totally different voice. "You can tell you've been out too long when the geeks start looking good. Knockers, ahhh—" His hand plays with her blouse. The man is unaware, Lorimer realizes. He doesn't know he's drugged, he's speaking his thoughts. I must have done that. Oh, God. . . . He takes shelter behind his crystal lens, an observer in the protective light of eternity.

121

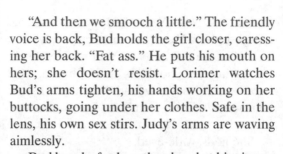

"And then we smooch a little." The friendly voice is back, Bud holds the girl closer, caressing her back. "Fat ass." He puts his mouth on hers; she doesn't resist. Lorimer watches Bud's arms tighten, his hands working on her buttocks, going under her clothes. Safe in the lens, his own sex stirs. Judy's arms are waving aimlessly.

Bud breaks for breath, a hand at his zipper.

"Stop staring," he says hoarsely. "One fucking more word, you'll find out what that big mouth is for. Oh, man, a flagpole. Like steel. . . . Bitch, this is your lucky day." He is baring her breasts now, big breasts. Fondling them. "Two fucking years in the ass end of no-place," he mutters, "shit on me, will you? Can't wait, watch it—titty-titty-titties—"

He kisses her again quickly and smiles down at her. "Good?" he asks in his tender voice, and sinks his mouth on her nipples, his

122

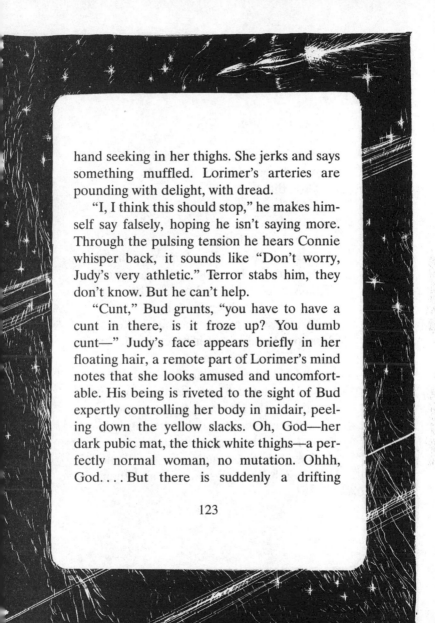

hand seeking in her thighs. She jerks and says something muffled. Lorimer's arteries are pounding with delight, with dread.

"I, I think this should stop," he makes himself say falsely, hoping he isn't saying more. Through the pulsing tension he hears Connie whisper back, it sounds like "Don't worry, Judy's very athletic." Terror stabs him, they don't know. But he can't help.

"Cunt," Bud grunts, "you have to have a cunt in there, is it froze up? You dumb cunt—" Judy's face appears briefly in her floating hair, a remote part of Lorimer's mind notes that she looks amused and uncomfortable. His being is riveted to the sight of Bud expertly controlling her body in midair, peeling down the yellow slacks. Oh, God—her dark pubic mat, the thick white thighs—a perfectly normal woman, no mutation. Ohhh, God.... But there is suddenly a drifting

123

shadow in the way: Andy again floating over them with something in his hands.

"You dinko, Jude?" the boy asks.

Bud's face comes up red and glaring. "Bug out, you!"

"Oh, I won't bother."

"Jee-sus Christ." Bud lunges up and grabs Andy's arm, his legs still hooked around Judy. "This is man's business, boy, do I have to spell it out?" He shifts his grip. "Shoo!"

In one swift motion he has jerked Andy close and backhanded his face hard, sending him sailing into the vines.

Bud gives a bark of laughter, bends back to Judy. Lorimer can see his erection poking through his fly. He wants to utter some warning, tell them their peril, but he can only ride the hot pleasure surging through him, melting his crystal shell. Go on, more—avidly he sees Bud mouth her breasts again and then sud-

124

denly flip her whole body over, holding her wrists behind her in one fist, his legs pinning hers. Her bare buttocks bulge up helplessly, enormous moons. "Ass-s-s," Bud groans. "Up, you bitch, ahhh-hh—" He pulls her butt onto him.

Judy gives a cry, begins to struggle futilely. Lorimer's shell boils and bursts. Amid the turmoil ghosts outside are trying to rush in. And something *is* moving, a real ghost—to his dismay he sees it is Andy again, floating toward the joined bodies, holding a whirring thing. Oh, no—a camera. The fools.

"Get away!" he tries to call to the boy.

But Bud's head turns, he has seen. "You little pissass." His long arm shoots out and captures Andy's shirt, his legs still locked around Judy.

"I've had it with you." His fist slams into Andy's mouth, the camera goes spinning

125

away. But this time Bud doesn't let him go, he is battering the boy, all of them rolling in a tangle in the air.

"Stop!" Lorimer hears himself shout, plunging at them through the beans. "Bud, stop it! You're hitting a woman."

The angry face comes around, squinting at him.

"Get lost, Doc, you little fart. Get your own ass."

"Andy is a *woman,* Bud. You're hitting a girl. She's not a man."

"Huh?" Bud glances at Andy's bloody face. He shakes the shirtfront. "Where's the boobs?"

"She doesn't have breasts, but she's a woman. Her real name is Kay. They're all women. Let her go, Bud."

Bud stares at the androgyne, his legs still pinioning Judy, his penis poking the air. Andy

126

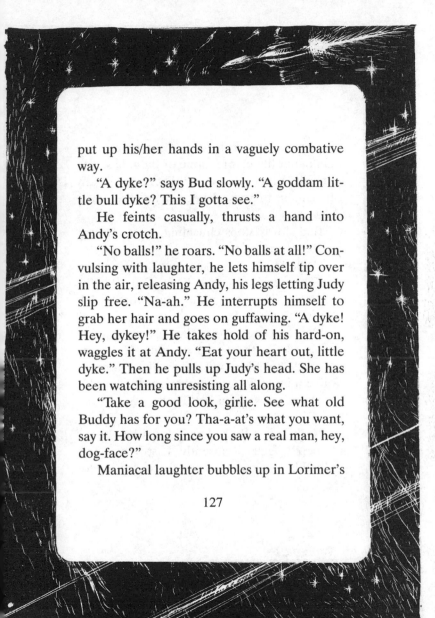

put up his/her hands in a vaguely combative way.

"A dyke?" says Bud slowly. "A goddam little bull dyke? This I gotta see."

He feints casually, thrusts a hand into Andy's crotch.

"No balls!" he roars. "No balls at all!" Convulsing with laughter, he lets himself tip over in the air, releasing Andy, his legs letting Judy slip free. "Na-ah." He interrupts himself to grab her hair and goes on guffawing. "A dyke! Hey, dykey!" He takes hold of his hard-on, waggles it at Andy. "Eat your heart out, little dyke." Then he pulls up Judy's head. She has been watching unresisting all along.

"Take a good look, girlie. See what old Buddy has for you? Tha-a-at's what you want, say it. How long since you saw a real man, hey, dog-face?"

Maniacal laughter bubbles up in Lorimer's

127

gut, farce too strong for fear. "She never saw a man in her life before, none of them has. You imbecile, don't you get it? There aren't any other men, they've all been dead three hundred years."

Bud slowly stops chuckling, twists around to peer at Lorimer.

"What'd I hear you say, Doc?"

"The men are all gone. They died off in the epidemic. There's nothing but women left alive on Earth."

"You mean there's, there's two million women down there and no men?" His jaw gapes. "Only little bull dykes like Andy. . . . Wait a minute. Where do they get the kids?"

"They grow them artificially. They're all girls."

"Gawd. . . ." Bud's hand clasps his drooping penis, jiggles it absently. It stiffens. "Two million hot little cunts down there, waiting for

128

old Buddy. Gawd. The last man on Earth. . . .
You don't count, Doc. And old Dave, he's full
of crap."

He begins to pump himself, still holding
Judy by the hair. The motion sends them
slowly backward. Lorimer sees that Andy—
Kay—has the camera going again. There is a
big star-shaped smear of blood on the boyish
face; cut lip, probably. He himself feels globed
in thick air, all action spent. Not lucid.

"Two million cunts," Bud repeats. "Nobody home, nothing but pussy everywhere. I
can do anything I want, anytime. No more
shit." He pumps faster. "They'll be spread out
for miles begging for it. Clawing each other for
it. All for me, King Buddy. . . . I'll have straw-
berries and cunt for breakfast. Hot buttered
boobies, man. 'N' head, there'll be a couple little twats licking whip cream off my cock all
day long. . . . Hey, I'll have contests! Only the

129

best for old Buddy now. Not you, cow." He jerks Judy's head. "Li'l teenies, tight li'l holes. I'll make the old broads hot 'em up while I watch." He frowns slightly, working on himself. In a clinical corner of his mind Lorimer guesses the drug is retarding ejaculation. He tells himself that he should be relieved by Bud's self-absorption, is instead obscurely terrified.

"King, I'll be their god," Bud is mumbling. "They'll make statues of me, my cock a mile high, all over. . . . His Majesty's sacred balls. They'll worship it. . . . Buddy Geirr, the last cock on Earth. Oh man, if old George could see that. When the boys hear that they'll really shit themselves, woo-ee!"

He frowns harder. "They can't all be gone." His eyes rove, find Lorimer. "Hey, Doc, there's some men left someplace, aren't there? Two or three, anyway?"

130

"No." Effortfully Lorimer shakes his head. "They're all dead, all of them."

"Balls." Bud twists around, peering at them. "There has to be some left. Say it." He pulls Judy's head up. "Say it, cunt."

"No, it's true," she says.

"No men," Andy/Kay echoes.

"You're lying." Bud scowls, frigs himself faster, thrusting his pelvis. "There has to be some men, sure there are.... They're hiding out in the hills, that's what it is. Hunting, living wild.... Old wild men, I knew it."

"Why do there have to be men?" Judy asks him, being jerked to and fro.

"Why, you stupid bitch." He doesn't look at her, thrusts furiously. "Because, dummy, otherwise nothing counts, that's why.... There's some men, some good old bucka-roos—Buddy's a good old buckaroo—"

"Is he going to emit sperm now?" Connie whispers.

131

"Very likely," Lorimer says, or intends to say. The spectacle is of merely clinical interest, he tells himself, nothing to dread. One of Judy's hands clutches something: a small plastic bag. Her other hand is on her hair that Bud is yanking. It must be painful.

"Uhhh, ahh," Bud pants distressfully, "fuck away, fuck—" Suddenly he pushes Judy's head into his groin, Lorimer glimpses her nonplussed expression.

"You have a mouth, bitch, get working! . . . Take it, for shit's sake, *take* it! Uh, uh—" A small oyster jets limply from him. Judy's arm goes after it with the bag as they roll over in the air.

"Geirr!"

Bewildered by the roar, Lorimer turns and sees Dave—Major Norman Davis—looming in the hatchway. His arms are out, holding back Lady Blue and the other Judy.

132

"Geirr! I said there would be no misconduct on this ship and I mean it. Get away from that woman!"

Bud's legs only move vaguely, he does not seem to have heard. Judy swims through them bagging the last drops.

"You, what the hell are you doing?"

In the silence Lorimer hears his own voice say, "Taking a sperm sample, I should think."

"Lorimer? Are you out of your perverted mind? Get Geirr to his quarters."

Bud slowly rotates upright. "Ah, the reverend Leroy," he says tonelessly.

"You're drunk, Geirr. Go to your quarters."

"I have news for you, Dave-o," Bud tells him in the same flat voice. "I bet you don't know we're the last men on Earth. Two million twats down there."

133

"I'm aware of that," Dave says furiously. "You're a drunken disgrace. Lorimer, get that man out of here."

But Lorimer feels no nerve of action stir. Dave's angry voice has pushed back the terror, created a strange hopeful stasis encapsulating them all.

"I don't have to take that anymore. . . ." Bud's head moves back and forth, silently saying no, no, as he drifts toward Lorimer. "Nothing counts anymore. All gone. What for, friends?" His forehead puckers. "Old Dave, he's a man. I'll let him have some. The dummies. . . . Poor old Doc, you're a creep but you're better'n nothing, you can have some, too. . . . We'll have places, see, big spreads. Hey, we can run drags, there has to be a million good old cars down there. We can go hunting. And then we find the wild men."

134

Andy, or Kay, is floating toward him, wiping off blood.

"Ah, no you don't!" Bud snarls and lunges for her. As his arm stretches out Judy claps him on the triceps.

Bud gives a yell that dopplers off, his limbs thrash—and then he is floating limply, his face suddenly serene. He is breathing, Lorimer sees, releasing his own breath, watching them carefully straighten out the big body. Judy plucks her pants out of the vines, and they start towing him out through the fence. She has the camera and the specimen bag.

"I put this in the freezer, dinko?" she says to Connie as they come by. Lorimer has to look away.

Connie nods. "Kay, how's your face?"

"I felt it!" Andy/Kay says excitedly through puffed lips. "I felt physical anger, I wanted to hit him. Woo-ee!"

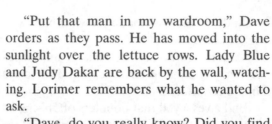

"Put that man in my wardroom," Dave orders as they pass. He has moved into the sunlight over the lettuce rows. Lady Blue and Judy Dakar are back by the wall, watching. Lorimer remembers what he wanted to ask.

"Dave, do you really know? Did you find out they're all women?"

Dave eyes him broodingly, floating erect with the sun on his chestnut beard and hair. The authentic features of man. Lorimer thinks of his own father, a small pale figure like himself. He feels better.

"I always knew they were trying to deceive us, Lorimer. Now that this woman has admitted the facts I understand the full extent of the tragedy."

It is his deep, mild Sunday voice. The women look at him interestedly.

"They are lost children. They have forgot-

136

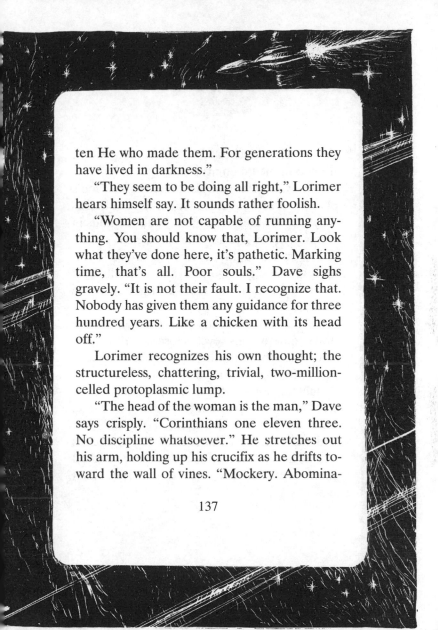

ten He who made them. For generations they have lived in darkness."

"They seem to be doing all right," Lorimer hears himself say. It sounds rather foolish.

"Women are not capable of running anything. You should know that, Lorimer. Look what they've done here, it's pathetic. Marking time, that's all. Poor souls." Dave sighs gravely. "It is not their fault. I recognize that. Nobody has given them any guidance for three hundred years. Like a chicken with its head off."

Lorimer recognizes his own thought; the structureless, chattering, trivial, two-million-celled protoplasmic lump.

"The head of the woman is the man," Dave says crisply. "Corinthians one eleven three. No discipline whatsoever." He stretches out his arm, holding up his crucifix as he drifts toward the wall of vines. "Mockery. Abomina-

137

tions." He touches the stakes and turns, framed in the green arbor.

"We were sent here, Lorimer. This is God's plan. *I* was sent here. Not you, you're as bad as they are. My middle name is Paul," he adds in a conversational tone. The sun gleams on the cross, on his uplifted face, a strong, pure, apostolic visage. Despite some intellectual reservations Lorimer feels a forgotten nerve respond.

"Oh, Father, send me strength," Dave prays quietly, his eyes closed. "You have spared us from the void to bring Your light to this suffering world. I shall lead Thy erring daughters out of the darkness. I shall be a stern but merciful father to them in Thy name. Help me to teach the children Thy holy law and train them in the fear of Thy righteous wrath. Let the women learn in silence and all subjection; Timothy two eleven. They shall

138

have sons to rule over them and glorify Thy name."

He could do it, Lorimer thinks, a man like that really could get life going again. Maybe there is some mystery, some plan. I was too ready to give up. No guts. . . . He becomes aware of women whispering.

"This tape is about through." It is Judy Dakar. "Isn't that enough? He's just repeating."

"Wait," murmurs Lady Blue.

"And she brought forth a man-child to rule the nations with a rod of iron, Revelations twelve five," Dave says, louder. His eyes are open now, staring intently at the crucifix. *"For God so loved the world that he sent his only begotten son."*

Lady Blue nods; Judy pushes off toward Dave. Lorimer understands, protest rising in his throat. They mustn't do that to Dave,

139

treating him like an animal, for Christ's sake, a man—

"Dave! Look out, don't let her get near you!" he shouts.

"May I look, Major? It's beautiful, what is it?" Judy is coasting close, her hand out toward the crucifix.

"She's got a hypo, watch it!"

But Dave has already wheeled round. "Do not profane, woman!"

He thrusts the cross at her like a weapon, so menacing that she recoils in midair and shows the glinting needle in her hand.

"Serpent!" He kicks her shoulder away, sending himself upward. "Blasphemer. All right," he snaps in his ordinary voice, "there's going to be some order around here starting now. Get over by that wall, all of you."

Astounded, Lorimer sees that Dave actually has a weapon in his other hand, a small

140

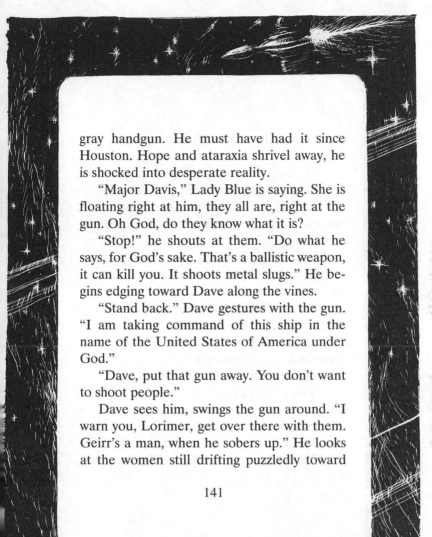

gray handgun. He must have had it since Houston. Hope and ataraxia shrivel away, he is shocked into desperate reality.

"Major Davis," Lady Blue is saying. She is floating right at him, they all are, right at the gun. Oh God, do they know what it is?

"Stop!" he shouts at them. "Do what he says, for God's sake. That's a ballistic weapon, it can kill you. It shoots metal slugs." He begins edging toward Dave along the vines.

"Stand back." Dave gestures with the gun. "I am taking command of this ship in the name of the United States of America under God."

"Dave, put that gun away. You don't want to shoot people."

Dave sees him, swings the gun around. "I warn you, Lorimer, get over there with them. Geirr's a man, when he sobers up." He looks at the women still drifting puzzledly toward

141

him and understands. "All right, lesson one. Watch this."

He takes deliberate aim at the iguana cages and fires. There is a pinging crack. A lizard explodes bloodily, voices cry out. A loud mechanical warble starts up and overrides everything.

"A leak!" Two bodies go streaking toward the far end, everybody is moving. In the confusion Lorimer sees Dave calmly pulling himself back to the hatchway behind them, his gun ready. He pushes frantically across the tool rack to cut him off. A spray canister comes loose in his grip, leaving him kicking in the air. The alarm warble dies.

"You will stay here until I decide to send for you," Dave announces. He has reached the hatch, is pulling the massive lock door around. It will seal off the pod, Lorimer realizes.

"Don't do it, Dave! Listen to me, you're

142

going to kill us all." Lorimer's own internal alarms are shaking him, he knows now what all that damned volleyball has been for and he is scared to death. "Dave, listen to me!"

"Shut up." The gun swings toward him. The door is moving. Lorimer gets a foot on solidity.

"Duck! It's a bomb!" With all his strength he hurls the massive canister at Dave's head and launches himself after it.

"Look out!" And he is sailing helplessly in slow motion, hearing the gun go off again, voices yelling. Dave must have missed him, overhead shots are tough—and then he is doubling downwards, grabbing hair. A hard blow strikes his gut, it is Dave's leg kicking past him but he has his arm under the beard, the big man bucking like a bull, throwing him around.

"Get the gun, get it!" People are bumping

143

him, getting hit. Just as his hold slips, a hand snakes by him onto Dave's shoulder and they are colliding into the hatch door in a tangle. Dave's body is suddenly no longer at war.

Lorimer pushes free, sees Dave's contorted face tip slowly backward looking at him.

"Judas—"

The eyes close. It is over.

Lorimer looks around. Lady Blue is holding the gun, sighting down the barrel.

"Put that down," he gasps, winded. She goes on examining it.

"Hey, thanks!" Andy—Kay—grins lopsidedly at him, rubbing his jaw. They are all smiling, speaking warmly to him, feeling themselves, their torn clothes. Judy Dakar has a black eye starting, Connie holds a shattered iguana by the tail.

Beside him Dave drifts breathing stertorously, his blind face pointing at the sun. *Ju-*

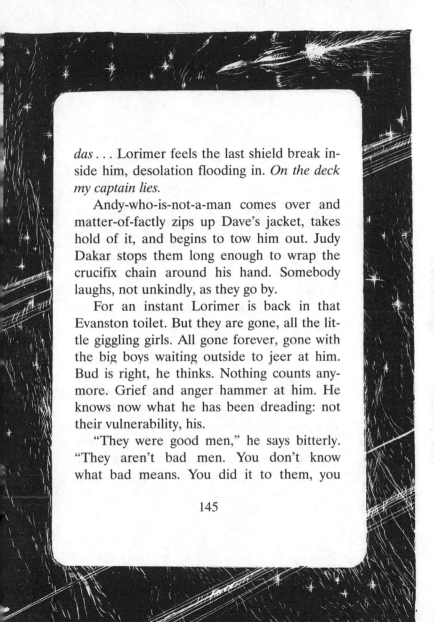

das . . . Lorimer feels the last shield break inside him, desolation flooding in. *On the deck my captain lies.*

Andy-who-is-not-a-man comes over and matter-of-factly zips up Dave's jacket, takes hold of it, and begins to tow him out. Judy Dakar stops them long enough to wrap the crucifix chain around his hand. Somebody laughs, not unkindly, as they go by.

For an instant Lorimer is back in that Evanston toilet. But they are gone, all the little giggling girls. All gone forever, gone with the big boys waiting outside to jeer at him. Bud is right, he thinks. Nothing counts anymore. Grief and anger hammer at him. He knows now what he has been dreading: not their vulnerability, his.

"They were good men," he says bitterly. "They aren't bad men. You don't know what bad means. You did it to them, you

145

broke them down. You made them do crazy things. Was it interesting? Did you learn enough?" His voice is trying to shake. "Everybody has aggressive fantasies. They didn't act on them. Never. Until you poisoned them."

They gaze at him in silence. "But nobody does," Connie says finally. "I mean, the fantasies."

"They were good men," Lorimer repeats elegiacally. He knows he is speaking for it all, for Dave's Father, for Bud's manhood, for himself, for Cro-Magnon, for the dinosaurs, too, maybe. "I'm a man. By God yes, I'm angry. I have a right. We gave you all this, we made it all. We built your precious civilization and your knowledge and comfort and medicines and your dreams. All of it. We protected you, we worked our balls off keeping you and your kids. It was hard. It was a fight, a bloody

146

fight all the way. We're tough. We had to be, can't you understand? Can't you for Christ's sake understand that?"

Another silence.

"We're trying." Lady Blue sighs. "We are trying, Dr. Lorimer. Of course we enjoy your inventions and we do appreciate your evolutionary role. But you must see there's a problem. As I understand it, what you protected people from was largely other males, wasn't it? We've just had an extraordinary demonstration. You have brought history to life for us." Her wrinkled brown eyes smile at him; a small, tea-colored matron holding an obsolete artifact.

"But the fighting is long over. It ended when you did, I believe. We can hardly turn you loose on Earth, and we simply have no facilities for people with your emotional problems."

147

"Besides, we don't think you'd be very happy," Judy Dakar adds earnestly.

"We could clone them," says Connie. "I know there's people who would volunteer to mother. The young ones might be all right, we could try."

"We've been *over* all that." Judy Paris is drinking from the water tank. She rinses and spits into the soil bed, looking worriedly at Lorimer. "We ought to take care of that leak now, we can talk tomorrow. And tomorrow and tomorrow." She smiles at him, unselfconsciously rubbing her crotch. "I'm sure a lot of people will want to meet you."

"Put us on an island," Lorimer says wearily. "On three islands." That look; he knows that look of preoccupied compassion. His mother and sister had looked just like that the time the diseased kitten came in the yard.

148

They had comforted it and fed it and tenderly taken it to the vet to be gassed.

An acute, complex longing for the women he has known grips him. Ginny . . . dear God. His sister Amy. Poor Amy, she was good to him when they were kids. His mouth twists.

"Your problem is," he says, "if you take the risk of giving us equal rights, what could we possibly contribute?"

"Precisely," says Lady Blue. They all smile at him relievedly, not understanding that he isn't.

"I think I'll have that antidote now," he says.

Connie floats toward him, a big, warm-hearted, utterly alien woman. "I thought you'd like yours in a bulb." She smiles kindly.

"Thank you." He takes the small, pink bulb. "Just tell me," he says to Lady Blue, who

149

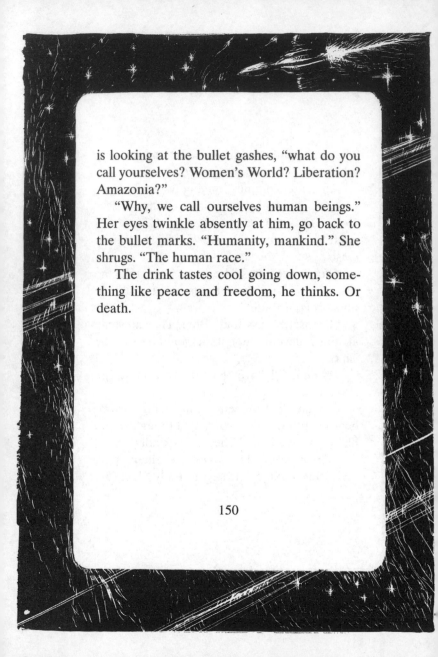

is looking at the bullet gashes, "what do you call yourselves? Women's World? Liberation? Amazonia?"

"Why, we call ourselves human beings." Her eyes twinkle absently at him, go back to the bullet marks. "Humanity, mankind." She shrugs. "The human race."

The drink tastes cool going down, something like peace and freedom, he thinks. Or death.

150

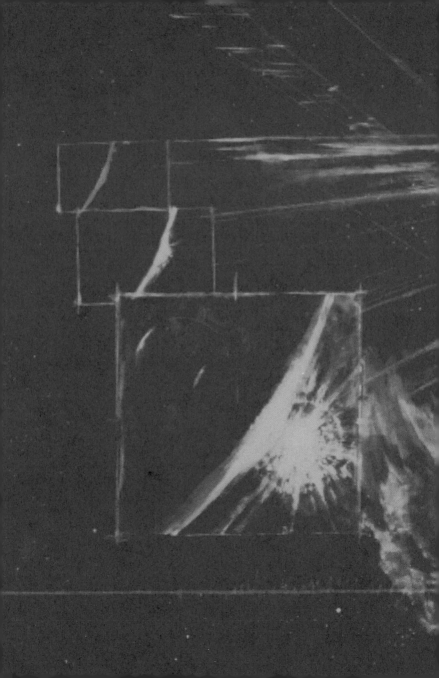